I0518321

Around Midnight

How to Write A Short Story in One Long Evening

by

Jack Lehman

CAMBRIDGE, WISCONSIN 2011

Zelda Wilde Publishing

Around Midnight

BY THE AUTHOR

POETRY
(Under the name John Lehman)

Shrine of the Tooth Fairy
Dogs Dream of Running
Shorts, Brief Poems of
    Wonder and Amazement
Acting Lessons
The Village Poet
To the Movies

FICTION

Geography of Sleep
Man with One Ear
Wolves beneath
    Chicago
Lit Noir
Men without Meaning
Tales Told in the Dark
    Shadows of Unseen Things
Goddess of Unspeakable Things
Lost on Clearview Road
Please Adjust Your Mask
Waiting for Dharma
The Angry Grandfather Chronicles
Not For You Kids
Downward Facing Dog
The All-Night Mystery Story
Sophie Tucker Speaks

NON-FICTION

America's Greatest Unknown
    Poet: Lorine Niedecker
Everything is Changing: How to
    Gain Loyal Clients and Customers
Write Angles
Write What You'd Love To Read
The Bark of Love

Around Midnight

How and Why a Poem Works
Around Midnight: How to Write a
    Short Story in One Long Evening
    Devil's Lake
The Trouble with Happiness
7 Days and 11 Nights: Writing a
    Novella for the Digital Age

PLAYS

A Brief History of My Tattoo
The Jane Test
The Writer's Cave
Last Day of the Sixties
John Jumps
Shadows of Unseen Things

COMPACT DISKS

10 Things I Think I Know for Sure
    about Getting Your Writing Published
The Writer's Cave: Why Writers Write
    What They Do
How and Why a Poem Works
    & Stopping by the Woods

JACK LEHMAN BIO

John (Jack) Lehman is a nationally published writer, poet and playwright. The innovative, approach he presents in this book is the result of his twenty years experience teaching creative writing and sixteen years as a creative director/senior copywriter for Midwest advertising agencies. He uses techniques from acting and film editing to unlock a writer's talent and give him or her the tools to produce stories, articles and books that move readers.

John is a graduate of the Great Books Program at Notre Dame University and has a Masters Degree in Curriculum Development from the University of Michigan. He currently conducts creative writing workshops and "Decisioneering" marketing/sales seminars for businesses, besides running Zelda Wilde Publishing, www.DamnGoodBooks.com. Lehman is founder and original publisher of *Rosebud*, a magazine for people who enjoy good writing and he was the literary editor of *Wisconsin People & Ideas* for many years. He is the author of six collections of poetry *Shrine of the Tooth Fairy, Dogs Dream of Running, Shorts: Brief Poems of Wonder and Surprise, Acting Les*sons, *The Village Poet* and *To the Movies*.

His nonfiction books include *Everything Is Changing* and *America's Greatest Unknown Poet: Lorine Niedecker*. His plays are: *A Brief*

Around Midnight

History of My Tattoo, The Jane Test, The Writer's Cave, The Last Day of the Sixties, John Jumps and *Shadows of Unseen Things*. They have been presented in Milwaukee, Madison and Saint Petersburg, Florida. His novels and short stories are on Kindle under the name Jack Lehman. Lehman has been nominated for the *Pushcart* prize in fiction, non-fiction and poetry and is the winner of the prestigious Christopher Latham Sholes Award from the Council for Wisconsin Writers. For more information about him, check: www. LehmanInfo.com.

Dedicated to my wife, Talia Schorr, and our wonderful life together with our dogs and cats in rural Wisconsin.

"Although John (Jack) is an accomplished writer, he is not one of those "how to write" gurus who deigns to deliver wisdom from on high. Instead he speaks from the perspective of a writer who struggles with works in progress and works yet to be created, while casting a reflective and critical eye on works completed in the past.

"He uses his own stories as examples, not because they are great works, but because by re-immersing himself in those stories and the processes of creating them, he brings himself much closer to the reader/writers who are striving to shape tales of their own.

"By providing simple structures and exercises that make it easy to begin and move forward with the story telling process, Jack is like the friendly local mechanic who will look under the hood of your story with you, and tell you what to do next.

"His book is a must read for anyone seeking to be a writer of short fiction."

— Roderick Clark, Editor/Publisher, *Rosebud Magazine*

"Jack Lehman's handy short-story writer's guide will appeal to both aspiring and established authors. The advice is rock solid ("Good writing doesn't tell us, it listens to us and allows us to do something life doesn't") and the writers and filmmakers that Lehman cogently discusses and dissects are first-rate storytellers (Raymond Carver, Patricia Highsmith, David Mamet, Andre Dubus, Orson Welles, Ingmar Bergman). Best of all, Around Midnight *includes six of Lehman's own powerful short stories and he shares their genesis and often deeply personal secrets.*"

— *Bob Wake, Cambridge Book Review*

CONTENTS

PREFACE

"Bounce on the board...and jump! "—Jack Lehman

I was teaching my first short story workshop. We were reading Raymond Carver and I invited the participants to talk about some object—the emotions or memories the pieces conjured up. The Carver short stories were "Cathedral" and "A Small, Good Thing."

In the first, a man who's blind asks another to describe a church by drawing a picture of it on rough paper. The blind man's hand rests on the narrator's pencil as he does this and later touches the impressions they have made. In our workroom Jack recalled that he himself was asked by a blind person to describe an elm. He happened to have a Bonsai tree so he took the man to his apartment and guided that blind man's fingers slowly over its trunk, branches and leaves.

Then Annie, a forty-year old who acted seventeen, when it was her turn, reached behind her chair and plopped a backpack on the table. From it she removed a fuzzy, cartoon-like duck. As she caressed the doll that someone had left at a Starbucks where she works, she told us, "My son died when he was six one summer at my ex-husband's house. Nobody knows what happened, only that they found him in the morning, a small rubber ball lodged in his throat." Her eyes look down. She straightened the bowtie on the duck. Then Annie unfolded the handwritten question pinned to its coat. It says: "Have you forgotten me."

You too need to tap into a personal dilemma. That's what you bring to the table this night of writing. You also need a structure that allows you, not only to dramatize this, but resolve it. At least for you.

Why do we have to have a structure? There are two reasons; 1) it allows us to suggest things that can't be put into words, and 2) this format is something others can read and respond to with their own comparable experiences. When that second part happens, it forces us, as writers, to do better, to be more exact...this time or the next. And mining the depths of something that matters to us is what good writing is all about.

I'll give you some tools and provide examples of how I have used them.

The short story has gone in and out of fashion, but the form itself offers you a unique opportunity to learn your trade—whether that is writing novels, plays, memoir and even creative nonfiction of any length. Many of our greatest writers, Hemingway, Faulkner, Fitzgerald and Henry James first became masters of the short story (as did contemporary writers, such as Joyce Carol Oats, John Updike, Tobias Wolff, Lorrie Moore and Charles Baxter). There may not be the money in a collection of short stories that there is in a novel or autobiography, but it is a form readily publishable in over 4,000 small magazines that can provide leverage for eventually getting a longer work published.

There's another advantage to the short story. A novel or piece of book length nonfiction is a world complete in itself. A short story is more like a spotlight that shines on a crowd of people. We see what is there but also know there are things to the left and the right of the spotlight that we can't see directly. These are the events of the short story that happen before it began or that will happen after it is over. As writers we have to plant clues for the reader and we depend upon that reader to create what isn't expressed. It's this partnering with an audience in the creative process that is invaluable for other types of writing. They depend upon it, but nowhere (except perhaps with poetry) is it more essential than with the short story. The secret of good writing is to get your reader actively involved doing the work for you. Writing short stories shows us how to do that. The words are important, but the story takes place beyond the words, in the imagination of the person who reads it.

Times are changing. Book stores and publishers are closing, but thanks to apps, hour-long TV programs, publish-on-demand (including one of my favorites—the novella surrounded by short stories), we are at the brink of a new short story resurgence. You can lead the charge.

Your goal is to grant wishes to your readers, disturb them or transport them. The short story is a great vehicle, but be warned of one thing, the good ones seem easier to execute than they are. I've often said I wished I could write like John Cheever but I know I can't. The genius of Raymond Carver is that he lets you think as you are reading one of his stories that, on a good day, you could have written it.

He lets us all be artists. Even my workshop participant, Annie.

How

CHAPTER 1

A Voice that Listens

People reading a book like this want to know what's first, what's second, what's third. I'm not sure what is second, third, etc., but I do know what is first.

You need to have at least three story ideas. Always. Never sit down at a computer or blank page of paper and think, "I wonder what I can write about?" Now there are good story ideas and bad ones. The good ones are about something you find unsettling, unresolved. You find answers through writing about them that you couldn't discover any other way, even by living them.

But here is the trouble. Most people new to writing feel insecure. They want to know exactly where their writing is going. They don't have confidence enough in a process that more experienced writers know works. But your reader isn't looking for the conclusions you have come to. He or she wants *discovery*, and finds an example in what you're doing if, that is, you are dealing with a subject that is risky to you and you are sincerely looking for answers you need to find. The reader wants that for himself or herself. Not your answers, their own. You are giving them a safe mechanism through which to do that. If you thought your writing was going to be about a subject you have already mastered, you are wrong. Good writing is a catalyst for the reader. Good writing doesn't tell us, it listens to us and allows us to do something life doesn't, under the guise of fiction or creative nonfiction. We can say, as we examine ourselves, I don't need to be afraid. This is only a story, only a personal essay, only…art.

A great story doesn't tell us something we don't know. A great story listens to us, allows us to hear ourselves in a way that we otherwise wouldn't. Why is this hard? Because that inner voice is sometimes alarming. Certain short stories allow us to feel things we do not dare admit. That's why we say writers *speak* for us. But they don't. Their work allows us to speak for ourselves. Their stories listen.

Let me kick off with an example. It is a story I wrote, somewhat based on real people and real events. The title is "How I Became a Writer" more aptly for you it might be titled, "Why I Became a Writer." Read the story and then let me use it to identify my story idea and some parts of it which I think you might find useful to your own story ideas.

How I Became a Writer

by Jack Lehman

When I was thirteen I was caught between the clutches of two aunts who hated each other. The one, Flora, looked like some old photos I have seen of Gertrude Stein, her stern face glaring at the photographer, her eyes shaded by a large brim hat. The other, Aunt Babe, did not have those angular lines, and her fire was within. In fact if you took a compass and drew a circle, then plopped two dots in it for eyes, you would pretty much have a portrait of this tall, 350 pound woman. We like fat people because they are jolly, right? Not so my aunt. She was married to a tough Irish cop, who was terrified of her. Now thirty years later I find myself wondering why it matters.

"Doesn't it make you think?" Aunt Flora, would ask me then when I occasionally found myself on her overstuffed couch with its white shroud (meant to protect the fabric underneath for special occasions, that never seemed to happen). "Here she is, supposedly happily married, yet getting bigger and bigger every day." Aunt Flora had

never married. Almost 40 years earlier, Flora, Babe, my mother and my grandmother had moved to Chicago from the small village of Rockdale, Wisconsin. My grandmother had bought this huge, three-story house where the four of them lived while the sisters attended college or trade school. When the other two sisters eventually married, and her mother died, Flora remained in the house, and, over time took in another woman from Milwaukee as a border. Aunt Babe and her new husband bought a more modest bungalow right across from them on Glenlake Avenue.

"She has nothing besides her teaching job and that musty old house," Babe would confide in me over pie on Sunday afternoons when I would bike over. "What a waste," she would close her eyes and shake her head. I'd watch her massive neck sway from side to side as I swallowed another bite of lemon meringue pie. "And that renter of hers gives me the creeps."

This was before the days when television became widespread, so each night of the summer, Aunt Flora would walk across the street to sit on the screened-in front porch with Dan and Babe. After dark, as neighbors walked by on the sidewalk near the streetlamp, the two women would call their "hellos," then lose themselves in the latest gossip about this person. It made for interesting conversation for both were excellent story tellers. In fact the two sisters were writers and had collaborated on four unpublished mysteries. That is why they interested me, for I dreamed someday of being an author myself.

 And my Uncle Dan was a valuable resource for their murderous tales. He could fill them in on police procedures and—these were the days of the original Richard Dailey as mayor—on some of the behind the scenes politics that made the city work. Once Dan took me to the police station where he was assigned and showed me around. He placed me in a cell and shut the door. It was to give me the feel of prison, but it scares me to this day. That clanging sound, no chance of communicating with others, being trapped, not only within a prison cell, but within yourself.

Babe and Dan had no children. They would spoil me with food and treats. The problem was that they didn't know what youngsters liked so I'd be showered with huge quantities of things I didn't want. For example, Babe's lemon meringue pie was unusually tart to the taste, but what can you say to a woman who bakes a whole pie just for you when she knows you are coming to visit. I told my mother about the pie, but for some reason she was perfectly satisfied keeping her distance from both of her sisters and was a little miffed that her only child would bother with them himself.

Once when I was small and my parents had to both be out of town I stayed with Babe and Dan over the weekend. In the top drawer of their dresser, when they thought I was taking a nap, I found my uncle's loaded police revolver.

Flora would write the background descriptions of their novels. "It was a rainy Saturday in April, small green buds, like caterpillars, had just started to appear on the outstretched bare limbs of the giant elm trees. A 1949 Packard slowly drove down the backstreet, its tires disturbing the mirror-like puddles of water stretching from the curb on one side of the street to the curb on the other. It was a pretentious sedan. The kind a short man might drive to impress onlookers…"

Uncle Dan drove a Packard. He said he would always drive a Packard. But when the car was wrecked and he discovered that the car manufacturer had gone out of business, he bought a Desoto (which also soon went out of business). He wasn't short. And he didn't drive slow. As if he were in a patrol car, he'd gun that sedan up to 50 between the stop signs at the end of each neighborhood block.

Babe didn't seem to mind Flora's words, because her dialogue about very masculine, female characters was equally pointed: "Now, now, my pet, you know how men are. That's why we ladies understand each other so well. Why we have things to talk about and know how to connect in bed."

The basis for these novels was never purely imaginative. There was always some story from the newspapers or spotted in a tabloid at the *grocery store that they agreed to explore. It was this aspect of writing that intrigued me. First, because they believed they were uncovering the unknowable by use of their intuition, and second, because I knew I could examine what they wrote and, using my intuition, discover a hidden truth about them.*

But there were other things going on at the time in my life.

I had recently recovered from scarlet fever. This took me out of school for almost half a year. During that time I was in bed, listening to the radio, drawing cartoon strips, reading anything I could get my hands on. I don't know if it was because I was lying down all day and drifting in and out of naps, or because of the fever, but when I did go to sleep for the night I would have strange dreams. Sometimes they seemed unrelated to anything in my life, but at other times it was almost as if I were visiting places, like my classroom or the drugstore on the corner of the large intersection three blocks away, and I was both there and not there—a kind of ghost. I remember once dreaming I was in the basement of Aunt Flora's house. It was after midnight and she was shoveling coal into her old-fashioned furnace. Blades of flame leapt out with every shovel full. She had a bandana tied around her head, and suddenly she turned and looked over at me in the corner. Her eyes glowed like embers. She raised the shovel over her head, like she would to kill a mouse, and started to walk over toward me.

I woke up, drenched in sweat.

Later that month Dan and Babe drove with his great aunt and great uncle to Las Vegas.

On the way his Packard ran a light and they were hit by another car. Great Uncle Charlie was killed. They returned and Great Aunt Annie faced a life of being alone. After I had heard about the accident I saw it in one of my dreams.

I was almost better by the arrival of summer. The worst thing about all of this was having to go to the doctor's office each week for a blood test. Even now my veins are difficult to locate under the skin in the crook of my arms, and I remember it was an ordeal back then often requiring several tries. School was over for the year, so for my first outing in nearly half a year I decided that on Saturday afternoon I would bike the eight or nine blocks over to see my aunts.

I walked my bike down the driveway and leaned it up against the fence along the alley by the garage. Then I walked back up to the front screened-in porch and rang the doorbell. I was surprised when it was Uncle Dan who came to the door. He smiled and invited me in, waving toward the outdoor-furniture love seat with woven metal back and hard plastic cushions. He had a glass of whiskey in his hand.

"Can I get you a ginger ale, Jack?" he asked. I noticed he had not shaved in several days which was unusual for him. "My Aunt Annie is sleeping upstairs, and Babe has gone out somewhere, so let's sit out here."

"Sure," I shrugged.

Dan disappeared into the house and a minute later emerged with a glass of ginger ale and coaster. He was smoking a Pall Mall. I noticed his drink too was now full.

"I suppose you heard about old Uncle Charlie," he started.

"Yes," I said. I didn't know what to say, really, and Dan seemed somewhat distracted.

"I understand you've been sick," he finally continued, though without much enthusiasm.

"I'm better now," I said, thinking that coming here had not been a very good idea.

Uncle Dan had a flat Irish nose and blonde hair combed straight back like that famous Dan of the time, the movie actor, Dan Duryea. It was strange to see him unshaven and not meticulously dressed. Theirs was an impeccable household where everything was always in place. Perhaps their lives had been this way too. Now, all of a sudden, they were not.

Around Midnight

"We were only one day away from Las Vegas. It had been a good trip. Uncle Charlie was sitting up front next to me but on the passenger's side. I don't know, there just didn't seem to be any traffic at all. Not like Chicago. In any case we had had an early start, before 7, had stopped for breakfast and later for lunch. It was about 3 in the afternoon, and hot."

"But you had air conditioning in the Packard?"

"Yes, that was on, but it was still warm. We were anxious to be at Las Vegas. I guess I was too anxious. I thought I could make the yellow light. It was out in the middle of nowhere. That's what I was looking at, that traffic light. I didn't even see the car coming through the intersection. He must have been going 80 miles an hour. He had the light, I don't deny that. It had changed. And then bang, we were spinning around in circles. When the car stopped. I couldn't believe I was all right and your aunt and my aunt were crying and screaming from the back. I knew they were all right. And I was all right, as I said. And then I looked over at Charlie. His head had cracked the windshield and he was slumped over, his head bent down. He wasn't moving and I knew it was all over."

Uncle Dan recited these words to me as if he had said them before. And it wasn't like he was really talking to me, but rather repeating them to himself. I took a sip of ginger ale. The ice cubes clinked against the glass. There was silence. And then I said words that I'm amazed at even today. It was totally untrue. I looked at Uncle Dan and quietly began.

"Several weeks after Mom told me about the accident I had a dream. And in that dream Uncle Charlie came to me and said something that I want to tell you. He stated that he was OK. He said that before he died he had discovered that he had cancer and that it couldn't be treated. He told me that had he not died in the car accident he would have suffered for many months. He was more afraid of suffering than of dying, and, as it turned out, he was spared from that."

Around Midnight

Whether or not Uncle Dan believed me, he nodded his head as if he did. Somehow the very possibility of what I was saying made him feel better. Or maybe it was that I cared enough to try and ease his guilt.

Later that year after he had been assigned to guard the stage door of the Auditorium, downtown, he brought back glossy pictures of Jerry Lester and the blonde bombshell, Dagmar, autographed to me.

THE END

CHAPTER 2

Make a Scene

I am using my own story (six others and three poems as examples throughout the book), not because they are better than those of authors and poets we admire, but because I have an inside track on how they developed.

I mentioned having a story idea, but that is not always as simple as it sounds. I find my best story ideas have two arms—a left arm and a right arm—and until I find these two sides of the dilemma I seldom am moved to start writing.

For example, with "How I Became a Writer," I did have two aunts who spent their evenings together, and each confessed to me (a pre-teen at the time) that they hated the other.

Years after they died, I had two elderly sisters in a writing workshop I was conducting in Boston who wrote mystery stories together. It was obvious that they too didn't like each other, but through writing (one did the setting, the other the dialogue), they were able to interact. Let me call that the right arm of the story.

The left arm involved my Uncle Dan, who was an Irish cop in Chicago. Tough, but a devastating incident happened that shattered his armor: he ran a red light outside of Las Vegas and as a result, his Uncle Charlie, was killed.

Without both of these, I don't think I could have written what I did. The magic thing is that in writing the fictional story I was able to regain part of my actual childhood (their house, my scarlet fever, the tragic car accident). But there is even more to it. I felt bad for my Uncle but never was able to express this. Now I am able to do that in the story. And, the made-up action is key to why writing worked for the two aunts and has for me over fifty or sixty years.

Why do we write? Why do you write?

Exercise 1—Earliest Memory involving Writing

On a sheet of paper write your earliest memory involving some incident with writing.

1. Describe the incident.
2. In a few sentences, talk about how you felt right before the incident.
3. Describe your reaction to the incident.
4. Talk about how you felt after that with regard to that reaction
5. Now, list some other possible responses you know (as an adult) you could have made then.
6. How would they have led to other results?

Returning to my piece, I said I didn't know what the second step of the writing process would be, but I do (step one is having some good story ideas): it is thinking in terms of the scenes to convey your two-armed story. For example, in "How I Became a Writer," there might be #1 a scene showing the contrast between the two aunts, #2 a scene in which they are working on something together and #3 the scene between me and my uncle. For planning purposes that would work.

A scene, as defined as far back as Shakespeare, is two people interacting at a particular time in a particular place. It has the advantage for the reader of grounding him or her. We can observe what is happening as if it were an experience we are having. The playwright, David Mamet, looked closely at the dynamics between characters in a scene. In giving advice to actors he says each character must have: an objective, an emotion, an action. If you think about it, this is like real life. One person wants one thing, the other wants something different and each will use whatever is in their power (words, body movement, facial reactions) to get whatever he or she wants. We, as audience, are curious as to who is going to win—that's why we continue to watch, or turn the page. And at the end of the scene, one of the characters wins and the other loses. Then it is on to the next scene.

The advantage to the writer is that the fleshing out of words, actions and emotions is for some purpose—to get a character to succeed. We aren't writing dialogue or giving description for their own sakes, but rather to help each character achieve his or her objectives in that scene. That's what plays on a reader's curiosity. Hell, that's what plays on ours. We keep writing to find out what is going to happen ourselves. But there is something even more. The scenes are like little mini-stories that stand on their own. Once we have written them we can decide how to order them so they create a dramatic arc: starting with a scene that grabs a reader and ending with one which is the best climax for the piece.

In life we may not want that kind of building tension (I don't), but in a piece of fiction it is the drama that a reader doesn't have in life that provides a punch and satisfies him or her by allowing them to experience emotions beyond what they would feel comfortable with in real life. Those heightened emotions define the boundaries of who we are.

So, you are a movie director picking locations, the characters who will be acting there and ultimately (after the shots are in the can) editing them in an order that builds from a beginning, to a middle, to an end.

Let me go back to my story to demonstrate that something comes from what is suggested earlier.

Scene #1 is actually two half scenes. Each of these highlights one of the aunts. The other character, the narrator in both, seems confused by their opposite qualities. Scene #2, also somewhat fragmented, shows the two women working together on a novel. More than anything else, it foreshadows how we project our own attitudes into our writing, whether that is through dialogue or setting. In other words, at the end the boy makes up a story which is fiction, but has a real connection to his uncle's tragedy. If in Scene #1 he is confused by the destructiveness and dramatic contrasts represented by the two women, in Scene #2 he is shown another possibility, how these opposites can work together for something positive. That leaves Scene #3, in which he must choose between fact and fiction in dealing with his uncle's grief. The unasked question with which I am confronting the reader is, "What do you choose? Do we sometimes lie, to tell the truth?"

But the answer, the resolution, is not the most important thing. Playing up the opposing possibilities is. In life we want to solve problems and quickly move on. In drama, we focus on the problem, build it with complications, make it nearly unbearable. Unbearable, so audiences have to confront, have to feel, have to re-examine their own lives afterwards in light of what they have just experienced.

Before we go on, let me ask you to do a second exercise. I will give you the characters and situation, but I want you to provide the particulars (from your own experience?).

Exercise 2—Fleshing Out a Scene

On a couple sheets of paper, try to write one of the following scenes. As you do this, role-play. Become each of the characters and do or say whatever you can to get your way. Author's are often accused of being schizophrenic. Here's your chance. Go nuts! If you are in a class or workshop, pick a partner and act this out before you write it.

A.

The scene:
A man and a woman are in a restaurant discussing the future of their relationship

Man's objective:
He is very upset because he fears that she wants to break up with him. He is trying to prevent this.

Woman's Perspective:
She realizes that she no longer loves him. However, she has some feelings for him and she doesn't want to hurt him. She is breaking up with him, but wants to do it as gently as possible.

B.

The scene:
A mortgage banker has just informed an applicant that her request for a loan has been denied.

Applicant's objective:
She has fallen in love with a house that she desperately wants. She is trying to convince the banker to process the loan.

Banker's objective:
This applicant's credit report shows a history of delinquent payments, and he just
can't take a chance on her.

C.

The scene:
Two hosts of a party have just said good-bye to their last guest. It's two o'clock in the morning.

Man's objective:
This person is exhausted and would like to go to bed now and leave the mess until tomorrow.

Woman's objective:
This person is wide-awake and wants to clean up everything and recap the events of the evening.

What if you are dealing with an emotion you have not experienced yourself. Mamet says we cannot fake it, an audience smells that a mile away. But there is a solution. It's called an "as if."

The "as-if" is there to get the actor away from the fiction of the script so that he or she can find parallels directly accessible to act on. Once the actor has used the "as if" to personally invest in a given scene, the lines and physical activities therein are tools to aid in executing the action.

Around Midnight

Mamet says:

> *The great debate throughout the history of acting is whether the actor must feel what his or her character is ostensibly feeling at any given moment. The bottom line is: What does it look like to the audience? The crucial thing to remember is that the actor is not on-stage to have an experience or to expose himself to the audience, but to help tell a story. At a certain point the writer may require and actress to sob over the death of the lover of the character she is playing. All that is necessary is that the audience believes you are upset (even if you substitute something else from real life that upset you).*
>
> *You may be playing a scene in which your character is dealing with his girlfriend, but your "as if" has to do with your brother. What the audience sees is someone with a need to get something from the other person in the scene, and it's understanding of that need will be based on the elements of the play, since that is the only information it has to go on. The audience comes to the theater set to believe the story. The actor comes to the theater to help tell the story, not by tricking himself into believing things he knows aren't true, but by applying the tools he has developed to create an illusion.*
>
> — A Practical Handbook for the Actor

CHAPTER 3

Use of Tools

1. Co-Journaling

I've been conducting and attending writing workshops for years, yet the best means for shaping my writing and making it interesting to others is something I discovered by accident. I call it "Co-Journaling."

This is such a simple thing. But, isn't it the simple things of life that we enjoy doing and appreciate most. This is especially true when doing them with another—cooking a nice meal together, taking a trip somewhere or even spending an evening talking about some subject that unexpectedly opens up our forgotten pasts. Co-Journaling is a simple experience two people can enjoy together with some bonuses besides.

In doing this over the past year, my wife and I have uncovered some guidelines that keep the process easy.

We sit down together at about the same time every evening (six pm). We write three or four nights a week. It helps to have a set time. It becomes a pleasant habit that is easier to do than not to do. By having a designated time we are almost always in the right frame of mind. Sometimes during the day I think of a topic I want to write about. Often Talia begins her thinking as she writes the words on the page. There's always something there, even if it doesn't come out for three or four sentences, and then we are off, just following where the words lead.

It does help to give your piece a title. It narrows the focus a little and, almost like a headline, sets the tone for the person hearing it later. Sometimes each of us will start with a title, often it comes once the writing has begun. Occasionally I've stuck one on just before reading my piece...well after the writing is done.

We write for about 20 minutes then stop. For some reason that seems about the right length of time, both for writing and for the length of piece you can enthusiastically listen to. If that isn't long enough, I continue it the next night and even a third (but reading the segment each time). It's as easy as stating, "to be continued."

Write in a location where you won't be distracted by the telephone or by kids' interruptions. I like the kitchen table; my wife prefers the couch. Later we meet on the couch to read. But make it comfortable and easy for yourself.

After we are done we read what we have produced to each other (this is part of the routine and not a matter of choice). We usually take turns starting. A lot could be said about this step, which is so different from keeping a private journal or diary. As it turns out this—not the writing—is the most important part. I'll say more about why in a minute. The reading takes about 20 minutes, total.

Don't think about correctness, about grammar or punctuation as you write. And don't worry about such things as being original or clever or trying to teach someone a lesson. The pieces I cherish most are the ones I did when I got all of these attempts to impress another out of my system. *Intellectualizing about a subject turns an audience off; making it a vivid experience from which a listener (reader) can draw his or her own conclusions, is a huge compliment. When you're writing from the heart, you'll be amazed how easy it is to write an emotionally compelling narrative.*

Another guideline is to each write in notebooks to be used for that purpose only. Whether or not you ever return to what you have written (and you will), it is a wonderful feeling to have everything together. I have gone back to type many of my pieces and share them with family members and friends, besides Talia. Some I've even sent out to be published. That's an extra benefit: once you get accustomed to sharing parts of yourself and your life with one person it becomes easier to do the same with others. And, you never know they may do the same with you.

Set a time frame for which you want to do this: three months, the length of a vacation together, every Friday night for a year, etc. When you have reached your goal, take a break. You'll come back to it willingly again, but don't make this an assignment or chore.

I think four things happen almost automatically when we read to a real audience. (a) It shapes the material, almost unconsciously. When we write for an audience there is a beginning, middle and end because we can see the expectation on the listener's face and in his or her body language; and we know what that person finds satisfying. We want them to be interested (the beginning), we want to clarify their understanding (middle) and we want to bring it to some sort of a conclusion (the end).

I feel (b) we are less self-indulgent with a real audience than we are in a diary—it keeps us honest. And, (c), this is the way we get to know the other person beyond our daily exchanges. I can remember how running out of things to write caused me to look back into the corners of my memory. Yet these are the "not so obvious" things that reveal who I am to Talia and to myself. Finally, (d) with each of these important or trivial things there is an emotion connected to it, so it's not only sharing our past hopes and frustrations but by sharing what we have kept inside we re-feel those emotions, unblock and release them. The purpose is not therapeutic or to gain sympathy. On the contrary it is a way to enjoy the very human process of mutual empathizing—of taking the time to listen to each other in a way each wants to be heard.

Pretty easy, right? All it takes are a pen, a notebook and a willingness to give it a try. But once you experience the result (and with Co-Journaling that happens immediately) you won't want to stop.

2. Storyboard

The second item is one we have touched upon briefly in the last chapter: the storyboard. The best way to explain a storyboard is to describe how it's used. Let's say we were going to do a TV commercial about a particular hotel. We are standing in front of the building ready to shoot, when the actor who is going to recite his lines positioned in front of the hotel says: "Wait a minute. I did a spot something like this a couple months ago, and instead of my just talking to the camera with the hotel in the background, after a few sentences the camera went inside and showed the viewer the swimming pool, restaurant and conference rooms I was describing." The cameraman pipes up, "Are you saying I have to drag my equipment from room to room in that place, it's not what I budgeted for." The lighting specialist is complaining he didn't bring the right kind of gels for indoors, and the sound engineer is yelling (he has earphones on), "Do you only want the talent's voice or also ambient sound in each of those rooms, or what?" It's anarchy...with everyone being paid a couple hundred dollars per hour. To alleviate this, before going on the shoot, the director creates something that looks like a comic script, called a "storyboard." It is a way of thinking through the creative decisions on paper—figuring out how the visuals and the words fit—before involving expensive actors and technicians in its execution.

As a writer, you're also in the words and pictures business, even if your pictures are verbal ones. And a storyboard, as we're going to do it, gives you a chance to make some of the creative choices before investing the time in writing them out. Have you ever agonized over something for hours only to discover when it was too late that another approach would have worked better? This saves you that frustration. Should you write without a structure or should you plot out the story and then write? The answer is you have to do a little of both (and get practice in both), but always be more willing to go where the characters take you than to try making them conform to a preconceived plan. Don't be firmly locked into a structure too early, no matter how inspired.

I'm going to give you an example, then ask you to do one of your own.

I start with three to five boxes in a horizontal line. In each I will put the situation the scene portrays. Below that box, I'll write the characters I envision being in the scene (and maybe in parenthesis, below these, the specific setting).

For the first block, I write "High School Kid Makes a Mistake." Under it I put "Bursey and Samuels." For location I am thinking of downtown Chicago where this incident happened to me." The next scene is many years later. In that box I put, "Bursey Interviewed for Job." Under it I again put "Samuels and Bursey." The location is a generic corporate office. For the final scene I write "Revenge," "Corporate Office." "Bursey and Samuels."

Now I am visualizing this as a completed story. I like the scenes, which follow a linear time-line, but wonder if it wouldn't be better to alter that. Start with the second block, and then at the end of the third scene do a kind of flash back to what was originally the first scene. There are some advantages to this. It throws the reader into the middle of the story and creates a double curiosity, where are we headed and how did we get here. I draw an arrow from my original first block back around to behind the last block. It is an explanation which fills out the third and represents the pay-off for the story.

In the next chapter you'll see the final piece, titled "Return Bout."

Exercise 3—Storyboard Exercise

1. Write down three story ideas.

2. Pick one of them and go through the same process we just did on this example for one of your story ideas. Use two to five boxes. Take as much time as you need to complete your storyboard. Do it now!

When you write, take some risks, let the characters say and do things without being sure where they will lead. Tell your characters, "Show emotion, listen to other characters, respond with honesty." If you don't have a subject you want to work with after all, go back and select a better one. It's more important that you write to understand your characters in their situations and the conflicts they face than it is to edit for an audience—that will come. The first step is to write, you can always go back to cut and paste later. You are going to do many revisions before you are satisfied, but not now. Don't worry about rough edges the first time through. Write fast! If a word doesn't come to you, leave a space. If something isn't going right, skip ahead, but keep writing without taking your pen from the paper or your fingers from the keyboard.

3. Director's Notes

Before you see my final short story, I want to share one last technique. I got this idea from a book on movie directors by Roger Ebert. He said that Spike Lee would work out his script/directing challenges in a notebook journal he kept specifically focused on the project at hand. In a way, this is talking to yourself on paper. I have found it very useful, especially for longer projects, like novels.

You are focusing on the challenge so that your unconscious can deal with it, and it does. You put a problem down one day, and the next morning you have a solution, almost miraculously. The other advantage director's notes offer is that you can get stuff out of your system that you then don't have to put in the story. Without that we tend to tell too much. We want the final product to show, but also hint at things below the surface (subtext). Work the subtext out in your Director's Notes, and leave it there.

CHAPTER 4

Think Quicksand

Let me give you an example in which using the third person I withhold information from the reader that is critical.

This story was fun for me for two reasons. I had a job interview for the position of director of the Wisconsin Academy of Arts and Letters that a friend had recommended me for. I felt uncomfortable because I have not had that many job interviews and, to be honest, I didn't know whether or not I really wanted the job. I left the interviewed really excited, not because of the potential job—which was, in the end, not offered to me—but because it gave me an idea for this short story.

When I wrote it there was another interesting bonus. The incident of the mail clerk had actually happened to me during a high school summer job. That was fifty-five years ago. Gone, but not forgotten. Finally I could get past that embarrassment by making it central to this "fictional" story. Nothing is ever lost, nothing is ever forgotten, but writing is a way in which we can take charge of situations where once we were the victim. Writers really do live twice, right Jack Bursey? The story, very appropriately is titled "Return Bout."

Return Bout
Jack Lehman

I am entering a boxing ring, he thought to himself as he walked through the door of the inner office and saw Mr. Samuels at his desk busy about little tasks, all of which were more important than interviewing him. Each of us, in our own way, is showing the other that he has been trained for this moment; but I know something he doesn't. Only one of us will leave this ring with his reputation intact.

"Now—Jack Bursey, isn't it?— sit down, please." Samuels waved the older man toward a chair in front of the desk. Only when the visitor had been seated did Samuels bother to look up. The room was uncomfortably warm for the first of April and there was the smell of an overripe banana.

"Before we begin, let me give you a little tip. The format of your resume is outdated, and you have left off crucial dates. Senior applicants sometimes do this in the hope that it will minimize their age. It accomplishes just the opposite. It tells me you think you are too old for the position."

The interviewee chuckled to himself. If he had had any hesitation before coming in here, if he had worried he might sympathize in some way with this conceited administrator, those feelings were gone. Good. Let the round begin.

"Have you actually had any experience working for a high-tech? I don't see that among all the other 'achievements' you've listed."

"Only one..."

Samuels looked dismissive.

"...which you might find interesting. T.C.P."

Samuels' head shot up as he said, almost involuntarily, "I worked there."

"I know."

"You can't be John G. Bursey?"

"Oh, but that's exactly who I am."

Samuels' face went red and a line of perspiration appeared along the top of his forehead. Samuels thought the other man's face looked vaguely familiar. Suddenly, his comfortable, square office seemed to be contracting. He could hear the tick of the battery-operated wall clock, the distant rumbling of the ventilation system. On his desk the chrome paper-clip holder, the letter opener, his antique stapler seemed dazzling in the ray of sunlight coming in through the half open window blinds.

And then he was back. Perhaps Bursey didn't know anything about that incident at T.C.P. Perhaps he himself was only imagining the worst. Perhaps.

"But that was then, and this is now," the job candidate smiled.

"Yes, yes, of course."

"Though…" The older man let the word hang in the air, and for Samuels the room again began to spin. "…I would feel a bit more comfortable sitting in your leather chair behind your desk, rather than in this vinyl, reception room chair."

"Yes, of course." Samuels smiled as if the other had made an interesting, though irrelevant, observation.

"No, I mean it. We will now switch positions. You will sit where I am in this molded plastic abomination, and I will sit where you are."

The younger man looked in astonishment as Jack Bursey rose. The man was serious. This was ridiculous. But… Samuels slowly got to his feet.

"Now that would be stupid, wouldn't it, young man?" the elderly man's eyes bore into Samuels.

They both sat down. End of the first round.

"Let me tell you something about myself that's not on that résumé. It's also why I'm here today," the visitor began as if the two had met seated next to each other on a long, evening airplane flight.

"Look, Mr. Bursey, I would like to hear what you have to say, but I just don't have the time right now. If you are the John G. Bursey of T.C.P., you are way overqualified for this job anyway. No. You're just not right for this position. Thank you for coming in. It has been an honor, as they say. Your time is valuable. Thank you. Good day."

"Being president of a large corporation can be anti-climactic in a way." the phlegmatic older man pressed the tips of his fingers together and briefly closed his eyes. Samuels swallowed. This was not going to be quick or easy.

"When you start a company you work eighty hours a week, doing whatever job you have to in order that things are done and done right. Then to sustain growth you suddenly realize that you have to bring others in to take over. The same one-man drive that got the company off the ground at the next stage starts to work against its success. So you delegate and try not to micro-manage the folks you have given responsibility to."

Samuels said nothing.

"All of a sudden you're dealing with board members and investors instead of people who do the real work. They ensconce you in a corporate headquarters downtown with a polished conference table and view of the city skyline. But the company is you, as much as a son or a daughter is you. And when someone betrays that, passes off some corporate resources as his own. Borrows against those resources…"

"Listen, Mr. Bursey, I had my problems too. I had a daughter who was sick, a wife who was unhappy, debts."

"Even if he gets caught and to save face the company covers for him and lets him leave as if…as if he had done his job. No, it still hurts years later. And when you retire and have nothing else to lose, you think, why not clean up the little affair? Why not see justice is done after all? Even if it is a small thing. Even if it doesn't matter to anyone at all except to that person who listed his T.C.P. experience so prominently on his résumé that he got an even better position at another high-tech firm.

Around Midnight

The older man sighed.

Jeffery Samuels felt as if he had aged 20 years in the last three minutes. His vision was blurred and his ears suddenly felt blocked with wax. He tried to sit up straight. He could smell the acrid odor of perspiration through his new Men's Warehouse suit coat.

"What do you want?" Samuels' voice was barely audible.

"I want the job."

"But why? Surely you make much more from your retirement plan and your stock options than this basic position could ever pay?"

"Not that job. Not the one you have advertised. I NEED JUSTICE. I WANT YOUR JOB. You see, Samuels, I do covet your leather chair."

After a moment Jeffrey Samuels began breathing again. Wait a minute, he thought. What can this guy do. He can't make me resign. There is nothing on my record that indicates any wrongdoing. This is all a hoax. I fell for it, but I don't have to. I'm not down yet, and I am certainly not out.

"All this is very interesting, Mr. Bursey, but entirely beside the point. I have no intention of giving up my position and, even if I should, there is no reason in the world that you would be hired to fill it. We have one opening and I am sorry to say that you are not a candidate for it. You're just not right for this position. Any further discussion is out of the question. Please leave or I will have my assistant call Security and they will escort you out of these offices.

End of the middle round.

The other man smiled but did not move.

"I'm serious, Bursey, go."

"Oh, I'm leaving, but I think there is one last little piece of information you should know. It's just a small detail. Maybe it will matter to you, maybe it won't."

"What. For God's sake tell me and get out."

"It's just that T.C.P. has purchased this company."

Samuels stared at the cherubic-faced little man. Was he actually wearing a plaid lumberman's jacket over his shirt and tie?

"That's impossible. I certainly would know it if that were true."

"Not necessarily. You see the take-over was kept relatively quiet. Part of the deal so insiders wouldn't start buying up stock beforehand. But by tomorrow it will be in the papers. And by Friday you'll be out looking for a new position. This time, I dare say, without such sterling references. For, besides feeling that little wrongs should be set right, I know that people do not easily change character. If someone were dishonest in one position they probably would be dishonest in the next."

That was somewhat true of Jeffrey Samuels.

And with that Jack Bursey slowly pulled a cigar out of an inside pocket and rose from his chair.

"How can I put this?" he said turning one last time toward Samuels. "You're just not right for this position. That's it. Samuels, you're just not right for this position."

As soon as the door closed, Jeffery Samuels went to the closet and took out his two attaché cases. He was not guilty of fraud, as he once had been, but there were certain irregularities that he would not want anyone looking into. For example, advertising job positions that did not exist to keep looking busy and important in his position as Head of Human Resources. The current owner might never suspect, but his old employer would be only too ready to investigate. He would clear out the contents of his desk, max the company credit card and head for California. The hell with it. By the time they caught up with him he'd have assumed a different identity or be dead. Since his divorce, things had been slowly deteriorating for him anyway.

Around Midnight

As Jack Jackson walked past Samuels' receptionist and headed to the bank of elevators, he pulled a packet of matches out of his pants pocket to light his cigar. He'd been a mail clerk at T.C.P. when the real John G. Bursey had still been its president. Now Jack was retired. In those days he'd delivered mail to Jeffery Samuels in-box. Four years, without so much as a "hello" from Samuels—the same person whose name he'd recently recognized as contact on a help-wanted ad. Once this Samuels had yelled at Jackson in front of the old mail clerk's fellow workers for dropping a letter as he hurried about his rounds and Samuels had later gone out of his way to insure the Jackson hadn't received a necessary raise. That had been thirty years ago. Jack Jackson would be the first to admit that he had never been very fast. But he was resourceful, kept his ear to the ground and wasn't above whiting out dates and re-photocopying an old Bursey résumé he'd Xeroxed long ago. Jackson never forgot Jeffrey Samuel's vindictiveness. Now he could.

Jack Jackson left feeling like a champ.

THE END

One of my favorite writers is Patricia Highsmith (*Strangers on a Train*). In talking about her writing she makes these observations.

1. Have two major (possibly conflicting) ideas within each peace.
2. Begin toward the end.
3. Emotion is key.
4. Most stories change ¾ of the way through.
5. First paragraph should be short.
6. First sentence—action, movement without the reasons for the movement.
7. Use dialogue sparingly to make it more dramatic.
8. Authors attract material they need when they are writing the novel.
9. See one or two scenes beyond the one you're writing.

10. Does the reader care about the character?

To start with, something needs to happen—muted, perhaps, delayed sometimes, or completely shattering—something which changes the status quo. The breakup of a marriage, the beginning of love, the death of an old man. And the author must find or imply some sort of solution.

The happening can be used in three ways. You can begin with it. Or it may begin with calm and existing order, proceed with rising intensity of the happening at the center, working back to a new order at the end—which is never quite the same as the old. Or you can withhold your ammunition to the very end leaving the reader to reassemble the parts for himself. I can't see the action taking place in "How I Became a Writer" anywhere other than at the end, but with some re-fashioning "Return Bout" did begin with the job interview and only at the end is the background of the revenge plot revealed.

In any case, the beginning of a short story should state the theme right from the very first line. This can be done by a metaphor or a passage describing setting that establishes the mood.

Plot never gets that complex in its development in a short story so a better term for what happens in the middle is a "complication" of the theme. It is the escalation of conflict between the results of choices that are presented earlier. The middle usually ends with the movement of the character toward one or the other of these, which leads to the climax at the end of the middle.

The end doesn't require a long summary of what happened afterwards as in a novel. The short story need only tell what happened and let the reader draw conclusions as to its significance for the character.

Don't make any drawn out explanations of the ending any more than you should do a lengthy introduction at the beginning. But the one unforgivable sin in writing is to be ambiguous. The reader may have to piece its meaning together, but it must be there to find.

Once you start to write your story, the next important thing is to finish it. Writing is as simple, and as difficult as that. An incomplete story is no story at all, while a piece of writing with all its faults can be a story if brought to some kind of an end.

Exercise #4 (do one of these two)

1. Write a dialogue of a couple of pages in which one person tries to seduce another. Make the seducer a fairly unlikely candidate for the job. Give strong motivation to your characters and this will intensify their speech. A dialogue that is motive driven is easier to write than a dialogue that has no apparent mission behind it. The stronger the reason for someone's talking, the more likely it is that you can drive the dialogue meaningfully. Or…

2. Write a dialogue in which two people argue intensely about something, and in the middle of the quarrel let them discover that they are both wrong. There had been some misunderstanding that in the quarrel gets exposed and settled. Then write the dialogue of reconciliation.

Around Midnight

Here is one of my favorite quotes about the short story by one of the real masters of the form. It is more than a quote, it is a plan of action. And it works.

> At my desk one morning I held my pen and hunched my shoulders and leaned my head down, physically trying to look more deeply into the page of the notebook. I did this for a moment before writing, as a batter takes practice swings while he waits in the on-deck circle. In that moment I began what I call vertical writing, rather than horizontal. I had never before thought in these terms. But for years I had been writing horizontally, trying to move forward; now I would try to move down, as deeply as I could.

> — Andre Dubus

When you begin a story and while you're reading it, it should seem as if you're moving from left to right: alternatives to the character's fate and to the plot's action seem open, possible, available. But when you've finished the story and look back, the action should seem inevitable, as if you'd moved from right to left.

But there is more to it than this. Writing is a kind of "sleight of hand" where the writer uses misdirection to sneak up on the truth. And the best way to manipulate the audience (as good as altering the order of scenes) is your choice ot point of vIew. In "How I Decame a Writer" I used the first person point of view. In "Return Bout" it was the third. There are some immediate advantages and a few real disadvantages to each.

In the first-person advantage "column," if we identify with the writer, this very easily becomes our story. We see, hear and feel what the narrator does, and if he holds something back we are justifiably angry. As a writer, even if we are slipping into a different identity, we are writing the story directly as if it were happening to us.

The disadvantages are: 1) Why should the reader want to identify with the narrator; 2) It is challenging to include background—why should I, sitting in my kitchen, which presumably I do every day, feel compelled to describe it; and 3) Most important, often what creates tension is the reader knowing something that the central character doesn't. We can get that easily using an objective (that is, third person) viewpoint from the thoughts and actions of other characters that the narrator is not privy too.

Point of view accomplishes two very important things. 1) Like a motion picture camera, it establishes the closeness or distance we as readers have from the characters. First person gives maximum intimacy. But we may not want that (especially if the character is very different from the reader and that kind of association will not seem natural). Third person objective (not knowing any of the characters' thoughts) is the most distant. It is the panorama, the historic sweep. Identifying with one of the third person participants and knowing only his or her thoughts is somewhere in between.

But that brings up the second thing point of view accomplishes. 2) It is not only a way of providing the reader with information it is also a way of holding back—we don't know what is on a character's mind. Such as, we don't know what is really on Jack Jackson's mind (in "Return Bout") until the end.

We must stick with our basic choice of first or third person for the entire story, but in a given scene we can alter the vantage point slightly from the other scenes, giving or not giving thoughts and dialogue or only giving one or the other of those things. Or another vantage point is describing only the action. We hold back so the reader jumps further in, imagining these things in a way which he or she will discover may or may not be correct.

When in doubt use third person point of view and write as if the story is happening in the past (that is a convention readers accept without thinking about it. The words of dialogue are always in the present so having the narrative be in the past tense creates a nice contrast that adds to the dynamics of the piece).

But the great thing about a short story, as opposed to a novel, is that you can easily try out different points of view and see for yourself which works best. But remember what Patricia Highsmith noted: For the reader to care about your story, there has to be something at stake—something of value to gain, something of value to be lost. Two strong forces are meeting, one of them triumphing over the other—for better or for worse. These may be "external" or "internal" forces or both. Tension in a story consists in something unresolved. Setting up something to be resolved and then prolonging or postponing that resolution is one way of putting tension in a story.

Sure, there will be introductory paragraphs, transitional ones, half scenes, but the majority of the story, no matter what point of view, needs to happen just as if a reader were watching and listening to it happen. It's built on talk and action. It's dramatized, shown, rather than being summarized or talked about.

Exercise #5

Take one of the sample scenes you outlined and jump in and write for thirty minutes. If at all possible make it one of the middle scenes of your envisioned piece (not the beginning nor the end). You want this to be an escalation of conflict between the two dynamic forces (characters). Something that brings additional consequences to the final choice.

I said that the reader can sense whether you are doing this or just rehashing stuff. This has to be a subject you have strong emotions about and, on paper, are not afraid to show them. You are doing this for yourself; you are doing this for a reader who feels he or she can't do it for themselves.

Take some risks. Surprise yourself.

You are a magician. Orson Welles once said,"There are no real magicians only actors pretending to be magicians. The actor performs hypnosis on a small scale that causes us to fall asleep into other worlds." A great writer is also a great actor who performs hypnosis. Causes readers, editors, teachers and some who are none of those things to relocate into his or her other world. And sitting at your computer in the dark, know the curtain is parting.

Hear applause start. Feel your spotlight. Write!

Who

CHAPTER 5

Writers as Vampires

In the section you have just finished, is everything you need to sit down and write your short story. This is how learning works. You get the basic techniques and the rest is hands-on practice, story after story. You get better. But there is more.

Not "how to" but "why." At some point you might look over what you are writing and ask the question, "Why do writers, why do I, write what we do?" The question is intriguing,…and the answer, liberating. Write, but when you feel ready, read this.

Question 1: Do writers sleep in coffins?

In the old days, victims of writers, e.g. readers, were occasionally interred while still in an author-induced deep sleep. This may have given rise to the myth from gravediggers and others who observed them emerging from coffins and crypts that literary people do sleep in coffins. So the answer is "no," though a writer may choose to sleep in a coffin for other reasons. I understand coffins are quite dark and very quiet.

 I had this idea for a one-person presentation from a DVD commentary on an Ingmar Bergman film, *Persona*. It suggested that a director/writer is like a vampire. *Wow*, I think, *the writer as vampire*. So I wrote something up. It began this way:

It is 35 years ago in one of the Slavic countries that gave rise to the legend of vampires in the 11th century. My first wife and I are wandering the streets of Split, Yugoslavia—an ancient Venetian city on the blue Mediterranean with white buildings stacked up its hills.

Around Midnight

I'd just left the Army and we were on the first leg of a year's journey that would take us to Greece, Yugoslavia, Italy, Austria, France, Spain, Portugal and back to Germany.

Anyway, it's a warm early fall afternoon and a crowd is gathering several blocks away. With our one-year-old in a carrier on my back, we hurry down the seaside street to see what possibly could be going on.

Even today, there's the snapshot in my memory that remains. A movie is being shot in front of an old hotel. This is intriguing in itself. But then we look past the actors and camera, we see that the man directing it is none other than...the legendary...

...Orson Welles.

He looks terrible. As wide as he was tall, he is dressed in a black shirt, black trousers, and a black suit coat that he must have slept in. His hair is greasy and hanging straight over his forehead and his corpulent face is a sweaty, beet red. He seems to be tilting slightly backwards to balance his colossal weight.

But it is THE Orson Welles. ORSON WELLES DIRECTING!

A taxi pulls in front of the hotel entrance and as the woman gets out the camera on the other side zooms in, shooting into the interior of the automobile she is leaving.

All this was done without any verbal direction. In fact this seems to be more of a rehearsal for a scene that will be shot.

Orson Welles turns to the cameraman.

My God, I am going to hear the greatest cinematic genius of all time actually tell his cameraman what to do.

He says, with that sonorous Orson Welles voice from deep in his diaphragm as if from the bottom of a huge, empty barrel,

Around Midnight

"Mario, keep your eyes on the camera, these people will steal anything."

That is it?

That is it. Probably no one in the crowd but Pat and I understand English, but we laugh all afternoon repeating the words: "Mario, keep your eyes on the camera."

And the baby laughs too...so hard and so beautifully that during the whole rest of the trip if we want him to roll with laughter, we say, "Mario, keep your eyes on the camera!"

What an anticlimax, but looking back what could he have said that would've been more memorable? For Orson Welles—known as the boy genius because of his early masterpiece, Citizen Kane—*making movies for TV in Yugoslavia was probably the low point of his career. And here was my son beginning his life…with wonderful giggles. My little boy's laughter was his masterpiece. To his parents, he was "our baby genius."*

A nice story, but now, almost 35 years later, here's why I think it fits the topic, "The Writer as Vampire."

As writers, we're consumed with finding significant "meaning." We are elated when we think we have that. But then times change. Life moves on. And what is significant, changes for us.

When I sat down to write a poem about the Orson Welles encounter 20 years later, my son was a teenager in the Air Force—neither a "teenage genius" nor an "Air Force genius," and my wife had left me. So the cheery ending of the little memory didn't seem quite appropriate anymore.

Around Midnight

Here are the last lines for the poem I came up with: *"Mario," he said, "keep your eyes on the people/ or they will steal everything."/And she did.*

My emphasis switched from watching the camera to "keep your eyes on the people." Now I had "truth" that fit my current situation. Did I forget that we had a marital property agreement, and at the time of our divorce—our kids had gone and the two of us were barely talking to one another.

SHE didn't steal anything from me. If anything, I was misrepresenting the situation for my own purposes. I was stealing from HER.

In his essay on the Orson Welles movie masterpiece, film critic Roger Ebert says of "rosebud," "it explains everything…and nothing." Who heard the dying Kane say the word before his death? The butler says, late in the film, that he did. But Kane seems to be alone when he dies; and the reflection in the broken paperweight shows the nurse entering an otherwise empty room.

Do writers, use events to mirror things that have a different meaning for them later on? Like vampires, take the blood out of the actual situation and transform it into something that gives them…what? IMMORTALITY?

QUESTION 2 : Will religious symbols ward off writers?

Holy water does not affect writers other than it gets them wet, and getting them wet might really aggravate them. The same is true of religious symbols. Simply holding them up in front of a writer will do nothing. Beating or hitting the writer with these religious symbols is a different story.

Around Midnight

I've learned, from years in advertising, to do a little test-marketing before jumping into projects with both feet, so when a publisher I've known for a long time asks me what I'm up to these days, I tell her I'm putting together a presentation called...

"Unearthing the Writer as Vampire."

 When she doesn't even slightly acknowledge this, I realize with a start that what I have is a "guy idea" that women (who are a high percentage of the writers I come in contact with) will not find intriguing. But is the subject restricted to males? I think about one of my latest experiences with writing and being published.

I was diagnosed with prostate cancer. Fortunately, I could get the treatment I needed through the VA Hospital in Milwaukee. But it did involve two months of radiation in which it was easier to stay there during the week . I thought, I'll use some of this time to write. About what? Oh yeah, having cancer, dying, the reaction of my wife and family to all this. My own reaction.

So I did. But I needed to address those heavy subjects gradually. My first inspiration was going down to the fitness room in the dorm I was staying at and striking up a conversation with the attendant, who was a pudgy fellow studying materials for an anger management class he was taking. It was an easy step to turn this guy in the basement into the devil and the fitness room into a kind of hell.

Next there was the endless waiting in chairs along the corridor in the lower level of the hospital for the daily radiation treatment. The people were nice, but after awhile I was tired of being the victim. I wanted to see them, not myself, in that role. Rationalized projection. Fun to indulge in, and actually fun to write. But I was getting closer and closer to a real wound.

My wife had her hands full with our dogs and cats at home and no one to help her while she was out doing landscaping, housecleaning and painting for income. What mattered most though, was that she seemed to be distancing herself from me. Later I learned from a friend, Rod Clark, whose wife had had breast cancer how devastating the thought of losing a spouse was to him. And another acquaintance I met in a writer's workshop, who had himself gone through several episodes with cancer, explained how others like to find you to blame so that they themselves don't need to fear the same thing happening to them.

My daughter wrote that she would come up from Florida to stay with me. I was touched, but in all honesty that would have caused more coordination problems than either me or my wife were capable of. As it turned out, for family reasons she couldn't come. But that gave me a real "ah ha" possibility. I would write this story up as if she did come (and maybe even through dialogue with her be able to say some things I found difficult to voice directly to my wife). Anyway, thorough this, I would face the reality of death.

I wrote "Going Down" and showed it to a couple of my male friends, including Rod Clark, editor/publisher of *Rosebud*. Rod liked the story and slated it for an upcoming issue of the magazine. Here it is:

Going Down

by Jack Lehman

1.

Paris glistens beneath a shimmering, mother-of-pearl sky. And the walls of the stairway from the second floor of the VA Hospital Residence Building are a light grey too.

The well-worn stairs only go to the ground floor. From there you have to walk down the dark hallway to an elevator at its end. It rides to the basement. There is only down.

And once you arrive, there is a restroom to the left and an open doorway to the right—from which comes a blast of retro music. The sign on the open door says "Fitness Room."

"Abe and Ida have been married for 40 years," booms the voice of a fat man with a red face. He is squished in a chair behind the desk to the right of the treadmills, in-place bicycles and stair-masters.

"What?" you ask.

"Abe is now retired. The couple bicker over seemingly insignificant things, like Abe never replacing the electric toothbrush and Ida spending too much time on the phone with friends and family. They go whole weeks without saying more than a few words to each other."

You look at the blistered face of the attendant. He is reading from an anger management handout.

"Can I use one of the machines?" you ask.

"What perspective are Abe and Ida coming from as they express their anger?"

Crosby, Stills, Nash and Young sing "What've You Got to Lose?"

Around Midnight

"Well, I don't really know," you offer. His face is now a bright red.

You mount one of the stationary bikes, start peddling, try to tell a joke: "Did you hear the one about the one-eyed fisherman? He caught a trout this big."—you hold only your right had up in front of your face.

"And are they being nonassertive, assertive or hostile/aggressive?"

You keep your eyes straight ahead on the Universal weight machine. "Listen I just came here to do some exercising. I really don't know much about these kind of things.

You smell smoke,

"And what about Mr. Magwitch in a George Webb restaurant. He orders a breakfast special that doesn't come. He starts yelling at the waitress? When she brings his plate he throws it on the floor. Storms out the door. Doesn't pay for his order. Or Sonny who suspects his wife of an affair? Or 11 year old Roy who does not follow his father's orders to go to bed?"

"Listen I just came here to exercise," you repeat. But it is more than that. You are a writer dealing with cancer. Dealing with a first-wife who has divorced you. A daughter, who became lost to you. A writer dealing with forever.

The attendant rises from his chair, tipping it backward. Hands planted on the desk before him, he bends forward and screams at you, "What about Carl-Sue sitting at three slot machines in the Up the River Gambling Casino? Blowing $200. Leaving the casino envisioning her ex-husband and his new wife enjoying themselves on a biking trip in France?"

There are shadows of flames on the wall of the small exercise room. Suddenly they burst from black on white to a fierce red blaze.

At the Luxembourg gardens, the faces of light-starved Parisians turn upward, like lizards.

Around Midnight

And you, down here, below, have only the memory of what the sun was ever like.

2.

Yesterday for breakfast we had chilled juices, rat-meal and Texas style French Toast with syrup. Rat-meal with warm milk and sugar. Yeah, rat-meal, not oat meal.

Cut-out paper hearts children had colored with stars and stripes are still taped to the wall from Valentine's Day. One of the four overhead recessed lights along the Radiation Treatment Hall blinks on and off, not related to the radiation machine, but seeming a little like lights dimming in movies where someone dies in an electric chair.

Today I check-in with Kathy who has a speech impediment and wait in unmatched chairs until I will be called behind the blue plastic curtain to the treatment area in the back.

Tonight in the dining room of the VA Hospital Residence Hall, called the Hospi-tel we are having celery sage bread dressing, Sonoma vegetable blend, jellied cranberry sauce and, on top of a mound of flat noodles, a brown gravy with what seem to be severed fingers and toes.

Kathy eats an apple and shakes her head unconsciously from left to right. A short black man in a maroon polo shirt, jeans and a new pair of Nike's pushes a cart up to her desk and places some brown envelopes in her outstretched hands. He reaches around the corner of her partition and takes the out-going mail from a metal wall rack.

Here is the remarkable thing. I have been coming here every day for three weeks. The second week I noticed something odd, but couldn't believe it. But this third week I am sure of it. Each of the people working here: Kathy, her assistant Daryl, the two registered nurses, a radiation technician named Claire Seeker, Resident Doctor Elizabeth Gore and Doctor Crawley are an inch or so shorter each week. I know, I know that sounds impossible. But today I watch Kathy's child-like fingers on the keyboard of her computer and they are definitely not as large as they had been.

The fourth week. Lunch on Tuesday is herbed pasta, roasted vegetables, sliced tomato salad with ranch dressing and more ragout of soldier. Did I forget the diced peaches in strawberry gelatin? Sorry. Now the employees of Radiation Treatment are easily six inches shorter than when I began. The other patients don't seem altered nor do they notice this astonishing change in height taking place.

"How are you doing?" Dr. Crawley asks me. There is a slight teen-age squeak to his voice.

"Fine, just fine," I answer.

Each day I go through the blue curtains, take off my shoes and pants and lie on a flat bed under the moveable arm of a linear acceleration apparatus. I pull down my pants and the nurse aligns my pelvis with three green lazars. Two from each wall. One from the ceiling.

High energy radiation penetrates below the surface. It is important that the oncologist work out exactly where the tumor is, so that the maximum dose of radiation can be delivered close to the tumor, sparing the surrounding tissue. There is no pain or heat or smell or noise. In order to make sure that the radiation is given to exactly the same place each time, it is necessary to make small tattoo marks on the skin

By the eight week, I align myself on the flat, narrow table and close my eyes. Hear squeals, like those of mice, as attendants scamper around below me. Or like those little people under the dumpster behind the restaurant at the end of David Lynch's Mulholland Drive.

And that last day… That last day I couldn't take it anymore. After, I was done, but before rising. I dropped the plastic ring I had been holding on my chest with both hands, and swooped my left arm down toward them.

Around Midnight

I grabbed the screaming attendants in my fist, scooped them up, stuffed them into my mouth and started chewing. Kathy, Daryl, the two registered nurses, Claire Seeker, Doctor Gore and, of course, Doctor Crawley.

3.

"How is he doing?"

"Fine. Fine. Well he is in a coma, but the vital signs are fine. Not to worry."

"Can I see him?"

"Better to wait here. I'm keeping a close eye on him. As soon as he stirs, I'll give him a minute or two, then bring you into his room. I'm sure he'll be pleased to see you. Pleased you are here. Help yourself to coffee."

On that last day, before he died, there were two things he remembered.

It wasn't Paris, but three in the afternoon and the sky was grey. She had just said that: "It's three o'clock, the sky is gray."

Later he wondered if this was all she felt or if she was trying to make it seem that way.

There had only been one time in his life when he felt he could be totally honest with others and with himself. It was that day when his first wife and he had come to the end of their (unsuccessful) marriage-counseling sessions. They sat on the steps outside of the man's office and she didn't care if what she said hurt him and he felt the same about her. They were getting a divorce and no longer had to pretend anything for one another. There was nothing more to lose.

That night he bought himself a steak and she purchased new sheets the following day. As months passed, all the nuances were lost. He acquired a set of Teflon pots and pans, she raked her garden and acted in a play. In years to come, the issues dimmed, then disappeared.

And the other thing? A series of stories he had written and wanted to perform called "Tales Told in the Dark."

He envisioned himself alone on a stage. Half way through his first piece, "You Are What You Dream"— a businessman seduced by a woman with a speech impediment and then caged in a Humane Society cell of doomed dogs, except it is a barrack with a bunch of men about to be sent off to Vietnam—the lights would dim and the audience would be listening to his words while sitting in the dark. Like people had listened to old-time radio drama with all the lights off as kids. Theater of the imagination!

Then there was "Sleeping with My Ex-Wife" which was actually about his adolescent daughter's first sexual experience. And another called, "Ghost Light," that told how his daughter and son, now adults, living down South, played an April Fool's joke on him. He had wondered, while he wrote it, about his daughter's distancing herself from him. And concluded it may have had something to do with his marrying a second time (not in the story, but in real life). And that was the final subject. His second-wife and he met after their deaths and read to each other what they would write. Perhaps the house-lights would come up as the two people realized this would be their eternity together.

But for now there was only darkness. Darkness and his voice telling strange tales from his life. They almost made sense, or would if he went over them again and again. He listened in the dark. Listened with his imagination. Like when he was a kid.

"Pop!" was all she said.

THE END

CHAPTER 6

And, Meanwhile

QUESTION 3: Do writers (who are known to stay up all night and sleep all day) burst into flames in sunlight?

Sunlight renders writers with their hyper-dilated irises, blind. It also causes neural pathways to fire randomly in the writer's brain, creating an extreme epileptic reaction. As dramatic as this reaction may appear, it will not be enough to start a fire, though some writers do sunburn easily.

Cancer treatment over (and by all accounts successful), I could return home and, no surprise, gradually block all of this trauma out of my life again. With one difference. Now I had something written that wouldn't let me completely forget. I would dump the "Unearthing the Writer as Vampire" and focus on the writing process with *Around Midnight.* No big deal.

But when the short story came out in *Rosebud*, my wife dismissed it (I wonder if she ever got past the first two somewhat fantasy sections or realized that the delirium at the end justified them and was a metaphor for my death). If I came across the piece in a magazine, I might have done the same thing, unless… Ah yes, unless they were something I had faced. And now from that new perspective I saw my story as a means to go, using Rod Clark's terms, "further in, further out."

I think there are different, identifiable stages to the creative process— from the first in which we absorb the world and its experiences through our senses and intuition, to a second in which our unconscious dreams and fantasies put these into a form we can handle,… through to an audience-testing phase and eventual publication or performance.

And what is the purpose of the journey?

To write stories and poems no one reads? Or to dig deeper and deeper…for example, to discover what death means for me?

It may be dangerous to do this with someone else's work, but as writers it is key to our uncovering greater depths in our own. In time, anyone can become a good writer; but to become a great writer, we must learn to become great readers of our own work.

My making Orson Welles central to that poem about my first marriage shows me that I want to "direct" my relationship with women. Not that this was a conscious process. As one writer says: "I try never to think about where a story will go. This is as hard as writing, maybe harder because I want to know what the story will do and how it will end and whether or not I can write it. But I must not know or I will kill the story by controlling it. *I work to surrender.*"

QUESTION 4: Are writers visible in mirrors?

This goes back to the Christian notion that any creature lacking a soul would not produce a reflection in a mirror. But, actually, with a few exceptions (and I think we all know who they are), writers are visible in mirrors, although interestingly enough, they are often quite discomforted by their own reflection.

In his 1966 movie, *Persona*, Ingmar Bergman explored the symbiotic relationship that evolves between an actress suffering a breakdown and the nurse in charge of her as the actress recuperates on an isolated, island cottage.

Around Midnight

As I watch it now, its implications haunt my life.

An actress—played by Liv Ullman—freezes up in the middle of a theatrical performance of *Electra*, thereafter refusing to speak. We aren't told why. She watches as the nurse, Bibi Andersson, chatters away about her troubled sex life. Then comes the weird moment on the screen in which the two women physically merge into one.

Bergman said that making the movie saved his life. Most of its significance, I believe, centers on the preoccupation with the two women's faces while at the same time transferring personalities between the mental patient and her lonely nurse.

For awhile the two women really seem to become intermingled. Suddenly, through the silence of the other woman, the nurse is able to put herself in that actress's place and understand the world with its senseless violence through the other woman's eyes.

That sounds much like something a writer would do, doesn't it?

I now live in the country with my second wife who one day meets a younger woman, Liviana, who resembles Liv Ullman a little. She is walking to town, a mile and a half away. At first she seems mildly retarded to Talia, my wife, but in reality she has a severe hearing problem. Liviana's speech is garbled and she consequently says very little. For some reason my wife thinks this is profound.

What I don't understand is that when my wife spends time with Liviana, she comes to believe that the silent young woman may have a spirituality she has been searching for in herself.

Around Midnight

All of her life, ever since my wife was a little girl, she has had a deep and profound love for God. She sees this as about changing consciousness in our lives and unhinging and un-limiting ourselves so that we can be all we can. She believes that ultimately that is the reality of God awakening in human form."

In any case...what **I need** to learn is something about Bergman and *Persona* or, even better, gain insight into the creative process.

Bibi Andersson had been Bergman's mistress, now Liv Ullman was assuming that role. The plot of the movie makes no sense in itself. Movie critics have been arguing over its meaning for nearly 50 years. But as a symbolic representation of Bergman's evolving relationship with the two women, it is as sharp and clear as a writer's image in a mirror. What we in the audience are seeing is not the characters played by Bibi and Liv but the artist's projection of his own feelings onto them.

...Is this just another case of a MALE projecting his feelings onto FEMALES?

Maybe, but maybe it's more, and it even goes beyond this film. What if a soul must navigate this world of suffering before reaching its ultimate destination? What if a person must embrace pain as intimately as someone would a lover? Meet pain and be annihilated by it? Make pain, illness, sickness and the diseases of humanity their own?

...To recognize this passage is necessary to the divine process by which all things are born, all things die, and all things are once more made new.

Around Midnight

I'm not talking about Liv or Liviana now, I am talking about something beyond them.

…One who steps forward, not to console, but to complete the devastation—to destroy all vestiges of false hope. What I have in mind is a female with fiery eyes, pointed teeth and a sharp, lolling red tongue.

She carries a sword in one hand which she wields with abandon. She lops off the heads of both angels and demons. She drinks the blood of the vanquished. All things are transformed in her and returned to the earth. They are rendered harmless in her…in time. She is time. She is Kali, destroyer of false hope.

She is the Hindu figure named for kala, which means "time"?

She was first born from the forehead of the goddess Durga during a battle in which this, the Great Mother, was called upon by the male gods— Brahma, Vishnu, Shiva—to protect the earth and all its inhabitants from the forces of evil.

Kali steps forward, not to console, but to complete the devastation that has already started.

Follow her into the mouth of the wolf. Through its enormous jaw. Past its razor teeth is a tunnel that leads down into darkness.

She is naked because she is ultimately pure and unashamed. And, she has three eyes in order to see past, present and future in one glance…to pierce through illusions. She is dark because she is not separate from the ultimate void out of which all things are born and into which all things die. Her tongue is extended because she desires blood and the life force of sex.

She wears a skirt of severed arms because they are instruments of power. And her hair is untamed, because each hair represents one of her followers, all of whom will run wildly in different directions trying to find their way back to her. We must chop off the head of illusion. Through art we must know that life and death are one.

In that original battle, Kali had not stopped with slaughtering demons. She continued her rampage, threatening to devour everything on earth. That's when the gods sent down Shiva himself—the lover to the Divine Mother in her many forms. Shiva laid himself down on the battlefield in Kali's path. She stepped on him. She felt his power under her feet. She stopped, looked down, smiled. The balance of the primordial Feminine with the primordial Masculine was restored.

CHAPTER 7
Finding Redemption

QUESTION 5: Can a writer be killed if one drives a stake through the writer's heart or chops off his or her head?

 Yes, but that would also kill regular humans if one does the same to them. By the way, killing a writer is murder and murderers are arrested and put in jail.

Each year I teach at a kind of back-to-nature folk school in Door County called The Clearing. Last summer in the short story workshop we read a story by Joyce Carol Oates called "Images" and I thought it might be interesting for all of us to write some scenes like she did.

Picture me standing up, addressing that class:

"So you see the problem in creating a scene between two people in a piece of fiction or creative nonfiction is getting into the mind of the second character—the one who is not a stand-in for you and your sensibilities," I tell the group.

Blank faces of the workshop participants stare at me.

In the workshop I continued, straight-faced, "I mean you have to become schizophrenic."

 No response.

"Crazy," I bellow.

 They laugh.

Around Midnight

The exercise I had given them is one from the beginning of this book: to write dialogue between two people in which one person—an unlikely candidate for the job—is trying to seduce another.

I tell the students, "You need to look at the motivation of each."

They give me blank stares.

"For example, in the Joyce Carol Oates story we just read, the adolescent girl—a surrogate for the author—wants to break loose from her family and the small town where she is going to school."

Heads nodin agreement. Who doesn't want to break out of their environment? Start a new life, not as someone else but as the real you who you never got a chance to be?

Back in the workshop a student objects, "But what about the pedophile teacher she is smoking cigarettes with?"

"Yes, what about him?" I repeat the question, using a teacher trick of responding to a question with a question in order to gain time to think of an answer.

"He should be reported to the authorities," Hugh pipes in. Hugh is a former grade-school principal.

"Well, yes," I say. "But that's why we have fiction, so we don't all wind up in jail. But in the context of the story what is his motivation?"

"He's just a loser," Heidi answers. She could be the story's strong female lead in a movie version.

Around Midnight

I stand at the podium, lost in thought. Finally I wonder to myself: Am I the loser? What the hell am I doing? Where am I going with this?

Getting a grip, I plow forward. And now?

Now as I think back on this incident, I remember some things I read in college.

Plato wrote about a cave in which the philosopher sees only shadows from a fire. He moves outside to discover truth in the blinding glare of the sun.

Freud gave this a literal twist—bringing our neuroses from their unconscious depths to the rational surface.

But wait. We may want to bring the truth out into the open but initially we need to go inward…into the writer's cave. It's there we will discover truth. When we do emerge it is the audience who will keep us from being self-indulgent and merely projecting our feelings onto other people and events.

Am I saying that when I change the encounter with Orson Welles and when Bergman's art searches below the surface to address subjects we need to bring out into the light…that this is some kind of terrifying journey?

Well, you are what you dream.

QUESTION 6: Can writers fly?

Despite being able to leap effortlessly from one subject to another, writers are not bats, but if they are on some kind of flying device like a plane or a helicopter, yes writers can fly.

Around Midnight

There are eight stages of the creative process:

1. In the first stage we absorb the world and its experiences through our senses and intuition.
2. In the second our unconscious dreams and fantasies put these in a form we can handle.
3. As we take ownership of the subject our empathy grows for the characters or people who are part of the story and we further invest our feelings in their conflict.
4. Next we make this tangible as a short story, poem, article, play or book, giving it dramatic structure that heightens those emotions.
5. Fifth, we test its effectiveness on others through classes, readings, and critique groups—clarifying, refocusing, reinterpreting.
6. In the sixth stage we incorporate that feedback into our project often mirroring a larger theme beyond our original scope.
7. We find an audience through being published or performing the piece.
8. And finally, encouraged by success we return to the initial stages and do more of the same at an even deeper level.

Or to put it more simply, you are what you dream. "You Are What You Dream" is the name of a short story I wrote last year.

You Are What You Dream
by Jack Lehman

When the twice-divorced John Larkin introduced himself at a downtown business card exchange to an attractive woman easily fifteen years younger than he was, he surprised himself by saying his name was "Jack."

She had a million dollars worth of tortoiseshell-colored hair, a soft, serious face and teeth that were even and strong and very white. She wore a faux fur jacket and skin-tight leather slacks. But her most unusual feature was one he could not see.

*John Larkin suddenly remembered twenty-five years earlier, the first day of boot camp. A man waiting in line, Skip, had introduced himself to John and John had given his name, "John Larkin." Moments later when they were joined by two other new soldiers, Skip had told them John's name was "Jack." He probably had had a friend, John, who went by "Jack" or perhaps—this was during the presidency of John F. Kennedy—he thought that the nickname was universal. It wasn't. But instead of correcting him, John thought, "Why not be Jack." It had a tough, aggressive ring he liked. Rash. And so for the month and a half of crawling under barbed wire, breaking-down and re-assembling weapons and binge drinking every Friday night he was "Jack." He could have been sent to combat in Vietnam. He even hoped he would be. But when reporting to his subsequent hospital administration position in Kansas, "Lieutenant **John** Larkin," was the name written on his assignment orders. And it once again seemed right.*

That's why, so many years later it was strange he would say his name was "Jack." But then he thought, as he had before, "Why not?" He knew the consequences of being "John"—the nothing person everyone dumped on. For once he wanted to be the guy who grabbed what he wanted.

Perhaps she was hearing impaired or had been born with deficient vocal chords, but the volume and tone of her voice was like she was holding her nose when she talked, or pronouncing words she'd never heard anyone else say. It was the voice of a cat that had somehow learned to speak

Cats are my business, she said. "Cass aaaa maaa bizzzz-nesss."

"I'm a dog person myself…" Jack was self-conscious. At first he had been embarrassed by the unexpected peculiarity of this woman's speech, now he was trying to show he wasn't. As he looked over the business card she had offered him, this was the best he could come up with: "It's not that I don't like cats. I do. But I've never had one myself. And I've never heard of a cat spa."

Then a strange thing happened. It was as if she were a silent-screen actress and the ballroom was flickering in black and white. Words, sound, didn't seem to matter. It was the look in her large eyes. It was seduction.

In a movie version it would have meant getting a room here at the hotel, ordering a bottle of champagne, peeling apart the crisp sheets and getting cozy under the covers of a king-sized bed. But Jack found himself in her feature, pulling out of the Sheraton's parking lot as they headed to the address of the Meow Spa and Cat Salon off of East Washington Avenue.

He smiled, remembering the old Steve Martin joke about how his cat enjoyed being bathed…though the hard part was getting the hair off your tongue afterwards. Maybe there was something kinky going on, but Jack was too horny to care. He wanted to press this little prize into the corner of a leather couch in the spa waiting room and pump the hell out of her while from cages in the other room cats in heat yowled.

The Meow Spa and Cat Salon was located in the old Humane Society building. Jack had been there once when his Norwegian Elk Hound wandering in the park had been picked up by the police. They had not called him and Jack had been frantic. Then the next day, to release the dog, the Humane Society was demanding he pay for its overnight stay. Jack had argued, "You never phoned me he was here. In fact I called and no one knew anything about Orson, my dog."

"The dog was riding in the back of the squad car most of the afternoon," the suddenly attentive woman behind the desk had tried to placate him.

"Humane Society, hah. What a joke. You people aren't good for anything except killing animals!" he'd screamed, and they had dropped the overnight charges.

But that rage was still there, Jack realized, as he pulled in front of the out-of-way building along the railroad tracks. All parking spaces for the Meow Spa and Cat Salon were empty.

She unlocked the front door and ushered him in. There was a small lamp lit on the ultramodern reception desk, the rest of the room was resplendent in art-deco shadows. There was no couch.

Here's what they teach you in the army, it's called "An Estimate of the Situation." Take stock of your surroundings, assess your existing resources, set priorities, act decisively, evaluate results. OK, Jack thought, there is no couch but the building seems to be empty of other people. Bang her and leave. Don't even think about this after it's over. However, one question did gnaw at Jack: How had she gotten to the business card exchange without a car?

The woman stepped over to a large metal door. She let her faux-fur jacket dangle and fall to the floor. Then she began to unbutton her blouse. Jack felt like he was again watching a black and white movie—but now it had become one in an ancient porn booths where you inserted a nickel and a pulsating Parisian beauty stripped off her clothes. This woman seemed to unleash all the wild desire he'd ever felt. She kicked off her shoes and was stepping out of her black-leather pants. There was a skulking, feline quality to her movements as she pulled one leg then the other free. She caressed herself and looked directly at Jack. He was staring at her breasts and at that inviting patch of fur between her legs.

Around Midnight

That's when he did something stupid. He hurried out of his own clothes as if he and she were two animals preparing to mate in the woods. And when he saw that Mary Pickford-look of slight alarm cross her face, he felt himself grow hard as a dog's bone. But before he could reach over to touch her, she had opened the steel door to the back.

Beckoning to him with her outstretched finger she slowly slipped out of view

Jack, completely nude, followed her.

When the door shut behind him, he felt a moment of panic. He was in some kind of hallway and it was completely dark. But he could hear footfalls of the little tease ahead of him and he had already seen all of her body he needed to.

The end of the corridor. Then there was a ninety-degree turn right. Down this hallway he became aware of metal bars on either side of him. He heard breathing.

"Uuuuu arrrr wha yrrrrrrr dreeeeam," her strange cat-like whisper seemed to summon him. He sensed he was standing in the entrance to some kind of enclosure. As he stepped forward he heard its door clang shut behind him.

War, to those who have never experienced it first hand, seems to be about noble causes. They imagine the soldiers who participate as exhibiting valor. But only people at a distance have the luxury of such sentiments. For men going into battle it is something else. Something less noble. Less rational. Something more real.

The fluorescent lights blinked on.

Jack saw he was in a barrack of naked men, like dogs in cages, smelling death.

THE END

Around Midnight

So what happened?
It's over. You've arrived.
So begin.

Why

CHAPTER 8

Ready, Set, Jump

Let me now indulge myself and review five benchmarks of my writing life. You may find parallels to yours or, if not, see that there are unexpected rewards that make this lonely choice worth it.

The first goes back to graduating from college (The University of Notre Dame) and deciding to go to California with my cohort, Dave Seaman, and become a beatnik. Of course we had read Kerouac's *On the Road* and it just seemed to epitomize everything we were not able to experience sitting in class rooms—taking tests, doing book reports late into the night.

We arrived in San Francisco to the realization we were ten years too late (that is a disadvantage of living in the Midwest, sometimes it takes a while for cultural trends to reach you).

Dave got a job selling encyclopedias and I delivered free newspapers with a bunch of alcoholics before sunrise. The rest of the time we lived in an unfurnished apartment, sleeping on a mattress-less Murphy bed and eating food Dave prepared with his boy scout cooking kit pan directly off of the counter without benefit of dishes or silverware.

After a month we moved on to further failure in Long Beach. But the last night before we left San Francisco we went out to the City Lights Bookstore. There for a few hours we were back in the Beat Era (I may even have bought an old copy of *Howl*). But wait, the best is yet to come.

Thirty years later (after stints in the Army, teaching high school, writing advertising copy) I decided to start the literary magazine *Rosebud*. We published the first issue and by some freak of coincidence I was sent out to Northern California to direct a commercial for American Breeders Service. I had an extra evening, and thought, for old time sake, I'd stop by City Lights.

It was still there and, and, and...on its shelves was *Rosebud*. I felt, as I have never felt before or since, that I had arrived. I was so euphoric that I bought all the copies that were there, despite having a couple thousand in my basement back home. Last year, we celebrated *Rosebud's* fiftieth issue. An accomplishment that almost rivals that bookstore moment, especially considering I originally had only enough money to do three of them. Let me commemorate this by a poem based on re-reading *On the Road* this year:

On the Road Again

It's Midsummer. You hike from Harlem
to Times Square and just as you arrive,

a great machine descends from the sky.
You awake, say good-by to your aunt.

Promise to be back. Take off for California.
San Fran-cis-co. Pan-fried chow mein,

soft-shell crab, steamed clams. Fog. Hills.
A clatter of empty cable cars. It's the sixties.

Coffee is only a nickel. Jazz, the Beats—all
that will never be "yes" again...are there.

Around Midnight

But there have been other equally astonishing benchmarks. A second happened at Fox Valley Technical College. I was giving a one day workshop and mentioned that sometimes we change facts to get closer to the truth of our emotions at the time we are writing about a subject. I used an example of locking myself out of the house. That had happened with my first wife, maybe 40 years earlier. It was interesting because I had to get a ladder and climb in, like a burglar, through the 2nd floor dormer windows on the roof. I went through the house and opened the back door to my wife. We laughed about it over a bottle of cheap wine that evening. But twenty years later, when I sat down to write the poem—we had been divorced—I changed the facts. Coming through the house, I wrote, I opened the back door and she was not there. That in some eerie way better fit my truth of the moment.

In any case, I found the poem and started to read it to the Fox Valley workshop. Here's what happened. I was just getting to the last two lines, when a woman in the back of the room recited them out loud. Oh my God! I was so shocked, I started to get dizzy. I actually thought I would pass out. I sat down in a chair and didn't know who or where I was. Nothing like this had ever happened to me before. Not only had she read the poem, but she had internalized it enough to make it hers.

Now, looking back, it reminds me of a short story I wrote based on a magic trick someone sent me on the Internet. Parts of the piece are factual. There was someone I once wrote an e-mail to who thought my message was from her dead boyfriend. The rest follows:

How the Trick Was Done

by Jack Lehman

You see six different cards on your computer. Think about one. Just one. Do not touch it. Do not click on it. I will find the card in your mind. Now look straight into my eyes on the screen. Think about your card. I do not know you. I could not see the card you have chosen, but I know exactly the card you have in mind. Look at the cards below. Now there are five. Your card is gone. Surprised!

Well anyway, here's what happened—this was after Sylvia had moved in and then a year later moved out.

Jack arranged a meeting with a woman he had known for years, in fact she had worked for him at one point, and he had always been attracted to her even though she was twenty years younger than him. "Eva" was her name. Thin body, long brown hair, dimpled grin. They met for coffee one afternoon and caught up on each other's lives. Jack told her about his failed relationships and she, in turn, told him about her partner of several years, Rob.

"He died last month. In the hospital. Of leukemia."

What do you say to that, other than, "I'm sorry"?

Jack had called her at her office, and she asked him not to do that again. He asked her if they might meet after work some night for a glass of wine. She said:

"No."

And instead of her home number, she did give him her e-mail address.

"That's the best way to reach me," she said.

To be honest, Jack felt she seemed indifferent to his attentions and he probably should have let it go at that. But of course he didn't.

Around Midnight

In the early days of e-mail everyone seemed to have a rather romanticized screen name. Hers wasn't but Jack's was. It was based upon the name of the hero in an aborted mystery novel he had written: "Messenger." Jack thought this clever at first, then incredibly corny. Eva hadn't asked for his e-mail address, nor was he inclined to give it out.

Jack compounded the situation by trying to be profound. In his e-mail to her there was no greeting, no small talk, just a saying from Zen Buddhism, which he had always liked for business: "Everything is changing. Everything is connected. Pay attention. From: messenger@aol.com."

That night she e-mailed back:

"Who is this?"

Jack's smart-ass reply, "Guess!"

How was he to know this Rob had been a Buddhist. That he had died on the same day and month that centuries earlier the Buddha had.

Her startling reply?

"Rob, Is that you?"

Jack needed time to think, but didn't. He simply e-mailed back. "Yes."

He immediately realized this was a terrible, thoughtless thing to do, but he was desperate. Jack wanted to be on the inside for once, even if it meant giving up his own identity and taking on that of a dead man.

And who did she see in the mirror of her computer screen: that hollow-eyed face staring back at her?

Around Midnight

"I'm so relieved," she typed. "Rob, there's something I should've told you but couldn't when you were so sick in that wheelchair, on oxygen, pushing food around on your plate..."

Each day we dress a certain way and speak words to others that are not us at all, but how others wish us to be instead. No, when we face ourselves in our mirror it's not a willingness to be deceived that we experience, but our willingness to deceive ourselves.

She continued, "I would have eventually left you, if you hadn't died and left me first. There I've said it. Forgive me, Rob."

If she were someone who you cared about, what would you do? How would you reply?

Jack wrote, "I forgive you, Eva. Of course I forgive you."

Jack figured out how to change his screen name, and that was that. Except it wasn't.

The more Jack thought about this the more he realized, if Eva believed she was talking to Rob, he had really been thinking, not of Eva, but of Sylvia. Others just mirror the tales of deception we tell ourselves.

That night as he fell asleep Jack realized, in that atmosphere of mutual resentment, had he been Sylvia he would have left himself too. But Sylvia was still part of Jack now.

The next morning he sat down and telephoned her.

When she arrived at his place an hour later, Jack showed her the David Copperfield Internet card trick.

"Look at the first set of face cards, and now at the second," she said. "All five cards are different from the original six. No wonder your card was missing. You were so focused on your own card that you didn't notice that."

Around Midnight

And, by God she was right, his missing, real-life, queen of hearts.

THE END

That one may take a little time to sort out, meanwhile here's my next benchmark. It is a bit more humbling. I had a man who worked for me as a sales executive. His wife was at the Wisconsin Department of Education. It seems that state agency had a multi-million dollar grant to study different types of intelligences and she hired me to interview teachers and guidance councilors at area schools. My report would be presented to principals and vice-principals at one of the high school auditoriums.

There we were all lined up on the stage before a full house of suit-and-tie public officials. My friend's wife started things off. She said, "This project is so important that we have even hired an outside writer. John Lehman, won't you please stand up." My mother would have been so proud, but just as the applause was dying down, a man's voice from the audience said, "Hey I know that guy."

All eyes turned to him (I recognized him as the principal of our local school). Anything to get beyond a somber, formal presentation. He arose. "My wife and I were strolling down the main street in Cambridge, and Lehman pulls up to the stop sign, in a red convertible, with three big dogs. Just at this time, a cute woman with her little dog on a leash comes walking down the sidewalk. All four heads in the convertible turned to give them the once-over."

Around Midnight

My creditability shot, I later went home and wrote the poem, "3 Three Big Dogs in a Convertible"—my consolation prize for never hearing from the Department of Education again.

3 Big Dogs in a Convertible

We're driving
down the Interstate
at seventy miles an hour,
the air…crisp,
cloudless and clear
except for one
sinister tear
wiggling its way
up the windshield.

The dog in back
is moving to the front,
the one in front is
moving to the back,
and a third
who was in front
then moved to the back
is now
sitting in my lap.

We're skiing
down the highway
through an ocean of rain
three heads of dogs
wedged
between windshield and dash.
There should be four dogs
in this car
and I, blinded and wet,
in bed
at home
with the cat.

Around Midnight

But the wall of clouds
brightens from behind
and opens
like a movie theater curtain.
I honk the horn.
We howl in delight.
There's more to life than
petty cares—
we're four guys in a car
cruising for girls.

I feel so happy,
I climb in back
and let the Labrador drive.

Let me tack on something that happened years ago at *The New Yorker's* Offices. When *Rosebud* first came out I had taken out a few minimum size adds in that magazine, so they were relatively nice to me when I dropped by. My daughter was attending NYU and I happened to see *The New Yorker's* name on an office entrance way. I thought, "What the hell!"

After I identified myself, someone behind the reception desk asked if I wanted a quick tour. A secretary took me around. What I'll never forget was walking past a storage room about the size of a football field, and her saying, "These are unsolicited submissions. We're waiting for the summer intern to come in and send them back with rejection slips." Summer intern! I had been sending my best poems and short stories to *The New Yorker* for almost 30 years. I envisioned Harold Ross or E. B. White pondering my work, eventually shaking their heads, reluctantly, and returning it in my S.A.S.E.

Around Midnight

Isn't it amazing how we anguish over something, send it in, and then when it is rejected say, "I knew I couldn't write description, dialogue. I'm just not any good." And all along it is the summer intern whose job it is, not to choose work, but send it back.

Last month I received a rejection slip from *The New Yorker* that had a hand written note on it saying, "We enjoyed these stories, Jack, send more if you have them." I don't care if it was an intern who wrote this, I framed it and have it sitting next to my computer. Probably more friends will see it there than read the magazine anyway.

My last two benchmarks are a little sad, and maybe more personal than the others.

When I moved to Madison, Wisconsin from Michigan. I gave up teaching to become a cartoonist. It was something I had always wanted to do. Sure, it didn't pay, but we had the money from selling our house.

My mother and father came from Chicago for a brief visit. Now my first wife was a good painter. My mother was a little disgusted with me for giving up being a teacher to be a cartoonist and my father, my father was suffering from Alzheimer's. He hadn't said a complete sentence for two years. Perhaps it was to cover this awkwardness that my mother started the conversation once we sat down to lunch with the pronouncement that, "Pat is a fine artist."

I'll never forget. My dad looked at my framed cartoon of a guy sitting in shallow water I had hung on the wall and said, "My son is a good artist too."

Around Midnight

Not exactly a writing benchmark, but I'll take it.

I was born the third child when my parents were quite a bit older. And once my sister, sixteen years my senior, sent me a photograph of mom when she was a teen ager. Months later I took my mother, who was in a nursing home, out to breakfast. I asked her about meeting dad and about her life when they were younger together. Now in her late eighties she dismissed my inquiries. "Oh that was so long ago," she said. "I don't want to talk about it. How about those Cubs."

No problem, I thought. I'll just use my observation, imagination and intuition to discover the story for myself.

CHAPTER 9

The Journey Home

The Journey Home

by Jack Lehman

"My grandson. Our grandson, and I can't remember his name."

The older man and older woman stood in the center of a small living room. To their rear was an entrance to the kitchen, where two men were talking. In front of them, a large bay window looked through an open porch at a cove.

"Don't worry," the woman said. I'll always be here to tell you. The things you forget, I remember."

"But…."

"Come sit over on the couch with me."

"But the breakfast dishes."

"They can wait. The boys are still at the kitchen table anyway, drinking coffee."

They both sat and for a moment viewed the water through the window. It was gray as slate. All the piers and boat hoists had been removed for winter. Soon the lake would freeze and someone could walk across its snow covered surface as if crossing Antarctica.

"What a summer, huh, Ed? But we made it. We made it."

"What?" The man was distracted.

"Sold our house in Chicago to the kids, and now with John and our grandson, Bobby, bringing all our things here to the summer place, we're done. It may have taken most of August and September, but it's finished." She was pleased how she had managed to work the name, "Bobby" into her answer. Giving him what he needed, without

seeming to. Was this what she would have to do? Isn't this what she had done most of her life? Suddenly she felt things were coming to an end and she had not yet lived.

"Done," she said. "We don't even have to unpack the boxes," Grace smiled. "We can leave them and go to the condo in Florida." She stopped a minute and then brightened up. "And you know what the best part is?"

"What do you mean?"

"We can stay with Lois and Bob anytime we want. For a weekend or a week or two. Back in our own house without worrying about its upkeep."

"It seems so cold out."

Grace looked at her husband and feigned concern.

"I know you miss being up here in the summer. Fishing, barbequing, remodeling projects."

"It's so cold and so empty."

Now she became defensive.

"It's the fall, Ed, all the summer people along Clearview Road have left. And we will too as soon as we turn off the water and electricity for the winter. The boys have put our things in the garage. We can get to them next spring."

The plan was that John and Bobby would head back to Chicago late afternoon and Grace and Ed drive to Florida at the end of the following week.

"Soon we'll be sitting around the pool with our old friends." she added without much enthusiasm.

There was the noise of chairs sliding back from the table in the other room and the clang of dishes being piled in the sink. Two young men entered the living room.

Around Midnight

 John, "Thanks for breakfast, Mom." He was forty, had a scruffy beard and wore a wool, lumberjack shirt. Beside him was his nephew, Bobby, twenty-six, in many ways a younger version of himself—but thinner, without the beard and a little more hip in Dockers and a black, turtle-neck sweater.

Grace looking at them both, suddenly self-conscious about sitting on the couch next to this man, her husband, remarked, "I wish you both could stay."

Once John and Bobby had been close. There was only a 14-year difference in their ages. But since Bobby's marriage and John's divorce they had drifted apart. This trip, in a way, was a chance for them to catch up. The preliminary chatter of the five hour drive there being over, they were both ready for more intense conversation through the dark night on the return. John made some excuse to his mother about getting the U-Haul back.

Bobby seemed a little self-conscious. He asked his grandfather about their coming up here to this cottage in the Upper Peninsula every summer. John had been telling him about it in the kitchen. It was Bobby's grandmother, Grace, who answered.

"That's right, Bobby, every summer. John and I would stay here and your Grandpa traveled up on weekends by train. He had some time off from work, but not the whole summer."

"By train, huh? That's cool."

Ed, conscious of the exchange going on around him, piped in, "And now John is married with children of his own."

"Divorced, Dad. Divorced. Bobby's the one who is married," John said.

"That's right, Grandpa, don't you remember? You were at my wedding."

Grace was a full-faced woman in her late seventies, with short grey hair she no longer bothered to dye caramel-apple brown. Ed looked

Around Midnight

like an old Warren Beaty might. He was still very angular, tall, with bushy eyebrows and swept back white hair. Jack saw himself in his father, like someone catching a surprise glimpse of his reflection when walking past a store window at night.

John, sat down across from his parents. He looked at both of them wondering what was going on.

John said, "We would go to the station around 10 on Friday nights to meet the train from Chicago." John and his father smiled. "I remember there was this crazy guy that was always on the platform shaking everyone's hand. We called him, 'The Mayor.'

"Then the engine would pull in and the passenger cars clang to a stop. The first person getting off was Dad. He'd have his suitcase, a newspaper and sometimes a box of candy for us. Remember, Dad? We'd come back here and you'd tell us everything that happened during the week, even what you'd had for dinner each night and what you'd watched on TV." John relayed these memories with youthful excitement.

Grace muttered to herself, "But I don't remember his asking much about our week."

John looked at her accusingly, "Why should he. It was always the same. Eating, cutting the grass, going swimming, sitting on the porch after dinner, going to bed."

Bobby turned to John, ignoring the others for a moment, "But why did they buy this place. Return to the place where they grew up? Be apart from each other for months every year after they had married? Why are they coming back to it now?"

* * * * *

It was during dinner that things started to fall apart. Grace had cooked a meatloaf with strips of bacon and gobs of barbeque sauce on top. She and Ed had a couple glasses of bourbon to celebrate and the boys each had two or three of the Coronas John had brought along.

Ed was lost in memories of high school in Menomonee.

"Remember the prom?" he asked his wife.

"We couldn't go together," Grace explained to the boys, "so Ed took a neighbor girl and I went with Fred, my older brother."

"Why couldn't you go together?" Bobby asked.

They were eating at a wooden table between the living room and the kitchen. It was next to an oil stove glowing with heat. Ed began rattling on about an ice-cream place that was once on Main Street with chrome stools along the counter. The high school students would go there to get sodas after school and listen to the jukebox.

Neither Ed nor Grace answered Bobby's question. John explained, "As you know your grandma is Catholic and your grandfather's family would have nothing to do with people they considered inferior. So that's why they couldn't court each other or even get married until both moved to Chicago."

Grace, with a faraway look, started to talk but it was not directed at either of the boys. It was almost as if she were reciting a story she had told herself over and over: "I moved to Chicago with my mother and two older sisters after high school. We all went to college, which was remarkable for three women in the 1920's. My oldest sister, DeDe, became a nurse for a large electrical corporation. The next in line, my sister Florence, got a job as a teacher of the handicapped. She never married and after DeDe and I moved on and our mom died Florence took over our house on Glenlake Ave. Ed had had a job offer by a company in Chicago that recruited boys taking drafting class at our little high school back home. The firm's president had gone to school there. So we got together, as people from Menomonee who had migrated to Chicago did in those days."

"And you were married," Bobby added with a smile.

"And we were able to get married in Chicago, whereas we never could have in Michigan. Married in the rectory of the church, like illegal immigrants."

Grace looked at John who she knew was no longer a practicing Catholic. "And now," she announced, taking Ed's hand, "we would be able to be married in a church, because as of last week Ed has become a Catholic.

The elderly man looked at his wife. He seemed bewildered.

"You mean," John gasped, staring at her, "now that my father has become senile you got some priest to baptize him?" John pounded his fist on the table and abruptly stood up.

* * * * *

It was after an hour on the road that night that Bobby finally broached the subject. They had left shortly after the early dinner. All cordiality had drained from the group with John's outburst. Grace and Ed were glad to see them go. Bobby and John were happy to be on their way.

"So," Bobby started, "what difference does it make if she bamboozled him into being a Catholic. They're both on their last legs. Let 'em do whatever the hell they want."

It had begun to rain. John drove. The empty U-Haul truck's windshield wipers slapped back and forth on low. He checked the gas, it was half full. Ok for now, anyway.

"When I was a kid, I always felt my mother thought she would have been a better business person than my dad. He liked people and did what he had to for the company. It was plush times for railroad equipment manufacturers and every year he got a bonus, and a promotion, and a new car."

"Well?"

Around Midnight

"And every year I saw my mother become more bitter. She was a good wife and mother, but felt relegated to those tasks. And being sent away every summer didn't help. It showed how non-essential she was to their success, in case she had missed the point. And now… Well the pendulum has swung the other way. She is in charge. Your Grandpa likes the idea of coming back to his home town. Sometimes I think he pretends he is reliving his life as if he had never left."

"And Grandma?"

"She is rewriting history, as she wants it to be."

"And what about you? What are you doing? Why did you get divorced?"

John was caught off guard. Did Bobby imply that John's over-reaction was because it mirrored something in his own life? John, so sure of himself, suddenly began to wonder if that were true.

"I don't know. I always thought Mom wanted me to be her stand-in in the world of business. That I would show the world the stuff I was (no she was) made of. Instead, I guess I was more like my father. Indifferent to success and drawn to a wife who was a strong woman like my mother. But there was one difference. I wouldn't take it. Or couldn't after a while."

"And you left her?"

"No, she left me."

"But if what you say is true…"

"It's true all right, but maybe that's why I'm upset about how my father is now being treated by Grandma. He's weak. I'm weak."

"I don't know," was all Bobby said.

In the years ahead John would find a wife who was a real partner, and Bobby, himself, go through a divorce then marry again. But that *night as they pulled into a truck stop for gas and a cup of coffee neither could admit one other thing. They had not been there for one another.*

At the gas pump there were cars going North and those heading to Chicago. Something about the orange glow of the overhead lamp and the gentle rain, precursor to snow, gave this a surreal feeling— like a station in the afterlife where souls were rerouted back to earth. All would arrive at their destinations with a sense of relief, maybe even new resolution, but tomorrow when the sun rose, the night's travel would be forgotten. Or if not quite forgotten, remembered in a shadowy way like a dream that some insignificant thing reminds us we have had the night before.

* * * * *

It was two days later that, doing dishes at the sink, Grace fell and broke her hip. She was sprawled there on the floor when Ed woke up from his afternoon nap. There were no neighbors left. It was winter in a summer place. He could have lifted her over to the phone on the wall. The service was still operational. That would have been the easiest thing. But he didn't and she, for some reason, never suggested it. Perhaps she was too proud, after all they had gone through, to ask for his assistance. Instead, he helped her to the couch. Then, as he had done nearly sixty-five years earlier at the prom, he brought her a coke.

"Someday you and I will be together," he began, "maybe after school is over and you go to Chicago and I go too."

"Ed, I used to want that, more than anything. And now. Maybe… Can I want it again?"

It was late afternoon. Leafless trees across the cove were like slender skeleton arms and hands reaching for a darkening sky. There were no sounds. No wind. No waves. Her pain was intense. In a few moments she would pass out. He would drive to the store, get some groceries and fill the car with gas. It would be two weeks before any of their children—not able to reach them in Florida—

would think to call. And then, when no one answered, notify the local police.

But now as Grace closed her eyes, Ed leaned forward. Was she dreaming of their future? He took her hand and rubbed it against his cheek.

In his mind, the band had started to play again. There was still time left for one last dance.

THE END

Being an Artist is a license to be yourself. And that's the high price also: finding and being yourself. For some it seems easy, for others it might take seventy years.

But that is what your audience wants, why they read, and pay attention to what you do: they want an example of how they can be themselves, and, at least for a moment, feel they have achieved this

Marshall McLuhan stated that the copy machine made us all into publishers overnight. After you've had some pieces published you will ask yourself, what is more important: To be in print or to be read? There are other ways in which you can share your writing that mean more than being in a national publication.

One instance of this happened to me nearly thirty years ago. I had been fortunate to have several dozen poems published over a period of a year and a half. My nephew, Bobby, who was an adult living in Chicago heard about this and asked me to send him some of my poetry. I Xeroxed a number of them and sent them off to him.

A month later he wrote that he had enjoyed them well enough, but that he was very surprised when his mother (my sister) came over one night and spent a couple hours in an easy chair reading them...one in particular. I instantly knew which poem this was.

Around Midnight

When I was about fourteen my sister and her husband were expecting their third child. They had decided to name it "John" if it was a boy. At that age I took this to mean they were naming the baby after me. The baby was born, right before Christmas. It was a boy. Unfortunately it lived for only a few days, then died. Everyone gathered at my parents home for Christmas Eve. Ordinarily my sister would have been in the middle of the celebration, she is very gregarious. That night she didn't feel like it so she sat in an easy chair in my room as I worked on the a model railroad building. I didn't know what to say. I still wouldn't; but years later when I wrote a poem called "Autobiography" it was this experience that was one of its central images. And now through writing my feelings expressed in that poem reached her.

No publication in a magazine could possibly compare to that.

A few years later I invited my sister to participate in one of my writing seminars. She had been a journalist and I thought it might get her writing again. When it came to the point where I talk about sharing your work, I thought to myself, should I include this anecdote. She and I had never discussed her child's death directly. I decided to go ahead and recount the story. When I finished all eyes turned to her, they knew she was my sister. She said, "You know the trouble wasn't that you didn't say anything, the trouble was that no one said anything."

I was so happy she had seen that poem. That she knew we did care, even if we couldn't say it. Later in the year, at another seminar, a woman called out, "My God, I had a baby, named John, who died and no one would talk about it either." We're all friends,...who just don't know each other. Writing is a way in which we do.

MORE

CHAPTER 10

Yard Sale

My sister dies first, then years later my brother. I was invited to his oldest daughter's second marriage and I couldn't help feeling I was him and time had moved on:

Anatomy of a Story

by Jack Lehman

How much detail should a writer include, what makes dialogue interesting, should there be a twist at the end of a short story? The answer to these questions is that we need to go deeper than these stylistic matters. Back to the underlying reason this is a story that has to be told.

"I'm not Tony, I'm Roland, his son."

"I'm sorry I didn't realize how much you've grown since I last saw you. I'm John, Tony's uncle. You look a lot like your dad."

"He's around here someplace, doing something for the wedding."

"Good, good. I drove in from Wisconsin for this and…well it's been a while since I've seen any member's of my brother's, your grandfather's, family."

"You were my grandpa's brother?"

"Yes, still am. I mean he's no longer alive, but I am. I just haven't seen anyone for awhile, being out of town and all, like I said."

And John knew that was the case for Tony as well. His nephew lived in Cleveland where he was a fire fighter. Ironically, Tony's was the last family wedding John had attended. John and his daughter had driven to it from Madison, Wisconsin, and stopped off in Ann Arbor on the way. John had gone to graduate school there and his daughter, Pamela, was considering doing her post graduate work at the University of Michigan as well. Now Tony and his wife had been divorced for many years and Tony's two children lived with their mother.

That was the curious thing about weddings. People go to them to be inspired, to praise everlasting love between a man and a woman. But what about second marriages like this one of his niece that John was now attending in the Forest Preserve of a Chicago suburb on a late Friday afternoon in June? As he looked at the front row of chairs set up by the gazebo for his side of the family, he could see that most of those who were sitting there were divorced, separated or the children of parents no longer together. Fortunately most of them had little tasks to perform: taking care of the rings, making sure the place cards on the dinner tables inside were correctly assigned, practicing a wedding toast or helping the bride get dressed.

John didn't see Mary anyplace before the ceremony. He guessed she was preparing for a grand entrance. As to the groom, he was anybody's guess. There were men in suits gathered at various spots throughout the garden. Any one of them would do.

OK, what attracts a writer to a particular subject? Being uncomfortable about a setting in which everyone seems to know one another and have something to do, except the observer of the scene? That, even more than why people join together and split apart, seems to be the answer. Creating a story gives a writer control over a situation he didn't have in real life. But now the characters and scenes are free to lead him beyond. He doesn't know to where. That is what is exciting to both reader and writer, because in fiction when fleshing out a situation, it is possible some deeper truth may emerge. Curiosity and risk become driving forces.

John thought about the tall gangling boy who had stood before him, wanting to get free.

Around Midnight

The boy looked like Tony, and Tony (when he came around the corner as they were talking) looked like a younger version of John. John's own adult children, as well as his deceased older sister's sons and daughters, had not been invited, and John's second-wife, Talia, and he had been in the midst of a major disagreement. She'd decided not to come.

Because John wanted to take pictures, he slipped to the side of the chairs and dutifully, after interminable electronic keyboard music, captured the big entrance, the rising for prayers led by a friend-of-the-groom's-family minister, and some quick words by an attractive female judge in requisite full-length robe. Then it was time for the exchanging of vows.

Mary: "I remember the afternoon at the country club meeting this man who'd been playing tennis with some of my friends."

This was nice. Personal, real. But then, behind the musician, through the bushes, John saw the face of someone who probably had not been invited—Mary's former husband.

"I realized, here is the man I had been looking for all my life, the man I was meant to be married to."

There was a loud crack. Like a gun. But it wasn't a gun, it was thunder. The sky clouded over and the world turned ominously black. The judge hurriedly wrapped up the proceedings. Within minutes the bridal party, attendant family and guests, robed judge, friend-of-the-groom's-family minister and John were scurrying through the rain like a gaggle of geese toward "The Grove," a bungalow-like reception hall where a beef and chicken buffet was to be served. The ghost of the former husband—real or imagined—had disappeared.

Let's say plot has moved forward. The setting mirrors the suppressed inner conflict of the narrator. So what? What's in this for me, the reader asks. Or for me, the writer might wonder. Why continue. But discovery in a short story is a vertical rather than horizontal thing. We don't find something

new, but rather how elements of the story that didn't seem to be connected at first, now start to fit together.

It was only when John saw the wife of his brother, Ed, and her sister that he suddenly knew. The sister, was grey, overweight and bent. She was talking too much, John could tell, even from a distance. He had known her first when they were both sixteen. She had dark Italian eyes and had had black hair she wore in a Bobbie cut. She'd been popular—active in school and church activities—and John, well he was a rather introverted nerd. But that connection wasn't what struck him. It was that his brother was not there. Often humans invoke those who have passed on, as if they were present in some way. Mary had talked about her father when John went through the reception line. But what really surprised John was when his other niece, Katherine, introduced him to her youngest daughter.

"This is your grandpa's brother, my uncle. Uncle John." And then to him, "Oh, I forget she was born after Dad died. She never knew him."

There is a wonderful photograph John remembered of Ed, his wife and all of all his young children, striding toward the camera, like the Kennedy's or something. Then his brother had died. Ten years earlier than even he, a diabetic, had expected.

Suddenly John was his brother returning. A stranger. And life had moved on.

THE END

So maybe your work doesn't sell, make you famous, even get read by those who are your family and friends? I don't know what the ordinary person would do, but the writer, the writer sees this differently. Like everything else that is perplexing, this too can be subject matter. And if you think poems aren't selling, let me tell you something. I had a yard sale and no one bought any of that stuff either. So I'm giving it to you. Both the yard sale and the poem.

But, seriously good luck with this. It's a way of life, that becomes its own reward.

Poetry Yard Sale

What if I took this poem and put it on a table
in front of my house, right on down there next
to the road. With English-class textbooks and
ski boots, a sleeping bag I never used and
that pottery mug. Would anyone pick it up? Even
if it were just a dollar or a dime or two cents?

Yet, it is what I have to give. This poem that
won't change anyone's life, but who knows.
And if someone did pick it up, and see infinity
caught between its lines, here is what I'd say,
"There are plenty more where that came from,
bud, today's your lucky day."

www.ingramcontent.com/pod-product-compliance
Lightning Source LLC
Chambersburg PA
CBHW070507130626
46555CB00003B/1188